PECOS
QUEEN

Other books by Barbara Spencer Foster

Girl of the Manzanos

Pecos Queen

Barbara Spencer Foster

SUNSTONE
PRESS

SANTA FE

© 2003 by Barbara Spencer Foster. All rights reserved.

No part of this book may be reproduced in any form or by any electronic or mechanical means including information storage and retrieval systems without permission in writing from the publisher, except by a reviewer who may quote brief passages in a review.

Sunstone books may be purchased for educational, business, or sales promotional use. For information please write: Special Markets Department, Sunstone Press, P.O. Box 2321, Santa Fe, New Mexico 87504-2321.

Library of Congress Cataloging-in-Publication Data:

Foster, Barbara Spencer, 1927–
 Pecos queen / Barbara Spencer Foster.
  p. cm.
 ISBN: 0-86534-391-8
  1. Mothers—Death—Fiction. 2. Young women—Fiction. 3. Texas—Fiction. I. Title.

PS3556. O7575P43 2003
813' .54—dc21   2003045552

Published in SUNSTONE PRESS
Post Office Box 2321
Santa Fe, NM 87504-2321 / USA
(505) 988-4418 / *orders only* (800) 243-5644
FAX (505) 988-1025
www.sunstonepress.com

Dedicated to my beautiful, talented,
and courageous mother,

Mabel Grace Autry Spencer

Foreward

Tererro is one of many ghost towns in New Mexico. It is located fourteen miles north of Pecos in the Sangre de Cristo Mountains on the banks of the Pecos River which heads a few miles higher up in the snowy peaks. Nothing is left to tell the story of this once thriving mining town. The large slag piles that slashed the mountainsides are now being removed as the mine site is being reclaimed.

I lived in Tererro from 1932 until 1939. My education started in the school the American Metal Company built for the children of its employees. It was situated at the bottom of the mountain on which the mine was located. The Pecos River flowed peacefully by the school.

Our family lived in a little village called Gifford Town. I was sure it was the most beautiful place in the world. Indeed, I had trouble adjusting to the less scenic lowland country when the mine closed, and we had to move away.

In Tererro's heyday there were 3,000 people who lived in the villages around the mine. Besides the main town which was located near the elementary and high schools, there were the villages of Chihuahua, across the river from Tererro, and Rico and Gifford Towns, which were on the mountain behind the mine. Indian Creek was another little settlement seven miles down the Pecos Road where the company sawmill operated.

I remember a post office, store, bar, and dairy. I remember the miners going to work climbing up the long wooden stairway that wound up the mountain to the mine. I remember going to watch the baseball games that were played on the ball park above Gifford Town. I remember searching for golf balls on the golf course right over the hill behind our little lumber cabin. I remember the school and the excellent teachers. Finally, I remember the aerial tramway that transported ore from the mine to a mill near Pecos. At that time it was the longest tramway in North America.

My father, Roy Spencer, was one of the last employees kept on the payroll after the mine closed. He worked as a security guard for the mining equipment until it was hauled away. He also kept an eye on the mine president's home, which was located in the pine trees above the mine and was surrounded by beautiful flowers.

Tererro still remains special to me, and I want to validate its existence beyond any doubt. Those of us who lived there, or are descendants of the hard working miners who toiled inside those mountains, will always poignantly remember the spirit and beauty of a place that could truly be called "God's Country."

Pecos Queen is a story about a young Texas girl, Grace Shockey, whose family came to Tererro because of her mother's health. The magic of the area creeps into her heart, but there are temptations beckoning beyond this pristine paradise.

Many of the characters in this story are modeled after unforgettable people I still remember in Tererro, but the happenings and events are fictitious, except for the strike. The miners went out on strike in 1936, and work resumed again after three months. Operations continued undisturbed until May, 1939, when another strike was threatened, and the mine closed permanently. Tererro then became a ghost town.

Many people visit the campground which is situated on the area where the original townsite of Tererro was located. There I went to school for seven years, walked up to the store for school supplies at lunch time, and mailed letters for my mother at the post office. If I had an extra nickel, I bought myself an ice cream cone at the confectionery.

Tererro was the site of my happy childhood, and I feel so fortunate to have known the inspiration and tranquility of such a place. I now live in a beautiful area in Montana, but my heart will always yearn for the incomparable ponderosa pines and the sparkling Pecos River in this beautiful mountain valley.

—Barbara Spencer Foster

2002

1

Liquid silver swirled around pink toes shimmering under the water trails of plump bugs skipping across the clear glistening plane.

A young girl sat at the edge of the river cradling her head in her hands as she contemplated the paths of the water creatures. "You're making rings for my toes," she murmured as she put one finger into the cold mountain water and watched the skipper bugs scramble to safety and immediately start their designs all over again. She raised her wet finger and pushed back dark silky hair which a slight breeze had blown over her eyes. As her hand moved across her forehead, she caught a glimpse of a figure approaching on her left. Thick black lashes swooped slowly over her smokey eyes in muted aggravation.

"Hi, Grace," came a high slightly nasal voice. "What 'cha doin'?"

Grace blew out a soft irritated sigh and opened her eyes to look up at the red-haired girl who stood at her side. Adele Johnson was tall and big-boned with clothes that hung on her in a chaotic and rumpled fashion while her hair snarled and tangled its way down her back. She looks like the Raggedy Ann Doll I got when I was a little girl, Grace thought.

"You got yore feet in the water," Adele observed. "You goin' to catch yore death o' cold." She put her hand into the water and quickly snatched it out and shook it. "That there water is mighty chilly, girl."

Grace stared at the red hand Adele waved in the air to dry. "Doesn't your mama have any lotion to put on your hands, Adele? They always look so chapped." She frowned and quickly turned away from the offending sight.

"Cain't afford it," Adele replied matter-of-factly. "I jest natu'ly have rough skin, I guess, like my mama." Looking down at Grace's smooth white hands, she continued, "It must be nice to have skin like yorn. But then, yore jest born lucky. Yore jest purty all over."

Grace's impatience with the big girl suddenly turned to compassion. She knew something of her family life. Her mother had told her that Adele had been born late in her parents' lives, and they had never quite figured out what to do with this surprise. Her father worked hard as a miner, and her mother cleaned cabins at a guest ranch, so they made enough money to buy food, clothes, and beer, and that was about it. Adele's mother humored and spoiled her, but she never worried too much about clean clothes or neat hair for her daughter.

Grace knew Adele had gone to school in Tererro all her life, but she had never developed lasting friendships and had gone her own solitary way until Grace entered the high school. Then she saw a chance to capture a friend before the other girls monopolized her. Grace didn't respond warmly to Adele's overtures, but she didn't totally reject her, either, so the two lonely girls formed a shallow relationship.

"Sit down," Grace directed. "I've just been sitting here cooling my feet and watching the water bugs. I guess I was envying them their freedom from worry and heartache."

Adele sat down clumsily on a big rock. "Yore heart hurts you, girl?" she asked with concern in her voice.

Grace patted her friend's rough hand and said with a slight smile, "I have a healthy heart, Adele. But, wouldn't it be nice to throw all your troubles into the Pecos River and let that beautiful stream take them away forever?"

"I guess so," Adele responded doubtfully. Sometimes Grace talked about things she really didn't understand. Anyone with good sense knew you couldn't throw your troubles in a river to get rid of them. Once you had them, troubles just pretty much stayed with you. That's what her mama always said.

Adele contemplated the river bank and picked a healthy dandelion growing in the moist soil. Changing the subject, she said, "Let's make some curls for our hair."

Now it was Grace's turn to be confused about what her friend meant. She watched as Adele discarded the thick golden blossom and divided about half of the stem into four parts. Then she put the divided stem in the water and held it there.

"What are you doing?" Grace asked as she pulled her feet out of the water and rubbed them on the grass to dry before she put on her stockings.

"You'll see," Adele said calmly. "Watch the stem in the water."

Suddenly the four tendrils started to curl up in perfect rings. When all four parts were tightly coiled, Adele took the stem out of the water and held it up. "See my curls?" she asked as she stuck the stem behind her ear. Four tight green curls peeked out of the stringy red wisps.

Grace was amazed. Noticing the admiration in the other girl's eyes, Adele said, "Here, you can do it, too, when you git yore stockin's and shoes put back on."

The girls happily made dandelion curls until they heard the school bell ring, signaling the end of the lunch hour. They jumped up to run to the high school building, but suddenly a tall shadow engulfed them. "Pick up that lunch sack," came the curt command from Miss Phipps, the principal. "If you're going to eat by the river, you know the rule: clean up your mess. We are lucky to have our school by the beautiful Pecos, and we are not going to ruin it with our garbage."

Miss Phipps' long arm and long finger pointed down to the offending sack. As Grace bent to obey her instructions she thought rebelliously, everything is long on that woman: her legs, her arms, her feet, her fingers, and certainly her nose. Then she straightened up, looked straight at the principal's nose, and said in a low voice, "Sorry, Miss Phipps."

"Don't let it happen again," came the order, and the girls hurried to class. But they didn't run fast enough to escape Miss Phipps' last direction, "And take those stupid dandelions out of your hair."

Grace and Adele slid breathlessly into their desks for English class, the last students to sit down. Mrs. Ellis looked at them with a smile. "Were you girls working on a Queen Elizabeth hairdo?"

Grace glanced at Adele and noticed she still had a couple of dandelion curls behind her ear. She deftly plucked the green coils from Adele's hair. "Did you all ever see dandelion curls before?" Grace was quaking inside, but she didn't know what else to say.

Mrs. Ellis smiled warmly. "Yes, indeed, I have made dandelion curls. They are beautiful and amazing creations. Someday you can give us a demonstration on how to make them, and perhaps you will also figure out the scientific explanation for what makes dandelion stems curl in water. That can be your speech demonstration project."

The other students were all set to laugh at these girls whom they had not yet accepted, and they were disappointed with Mrs. Ellis' reaction. They knew she would never put up with their negative remarks now. One boy, Ramon, a Spanish boy who sat behind Grace, whispered softly, "Can't wait for you all to show me how to make a dandelion curl, Tex." The students teased Grace about her West Texas drawl, but for some reason this remark sounded almost friendly. Grace turned slightly and raised an eyebrow at the mischievous smile on her neighbor's face.

"We will diagram this sentence, class." Mrs. Ellis' brisk voice demanded attention as she turned to the black board and wrote, "Dandelion stems make beautiful curls." Grace looked at Adele and smiled reassuringly. She appreciated the way the teacher was handling their dandelion dilemma.

Diagraming sentences was easy for Grace, but it was impossible for Adele. So Grace pushed her paper to the edge of the desk for Adele to glance at while she looked out the window at the bright New Mexico sky. I'm so glad the long cold winter is over, she thought. Maybe Mama will feel better now. She just has to improve in this warm pure air.

Thoughts of better health were interrupted by Mrs. Ellis' voice. "Grace, come to the board and diagram the sentence the way you did on your paper."

Grace slowly rose from her desk, a tall slender girl whose long black hair swung in graceful rhythm to her steps as she walked to the front of the room. She quickly drew her diagram lines and wrote the words in their proper places.

"That's correct," Mrs. Ellis pronounced. "By the way, your writing is lovely. Do you like to draw?"

"Yes," Grace answered softly. Then, lifting her head purposefully, she said, "I love to draw horses."

Mrs. Ellis smiled and looked at the class. "Isn't it nice to have a new girl in school who not only knows how to diagram sentences, but who also likes to draw? You must show us some of your drawings, Grace. And you can illustrate the stories you write. You are so lucky."

Grace's face flushed with pleasure as she returned to her desk. Maybe this school isn't so bad after all, she thought. When she had come here in the fall as a transfer student from Texas, she had thought she would never be able to adjust to the new teachers and students. Everyone was so different from her school in the small town where she had previously lived. Now as Mrs. Ellis smiled at her, she felt a warmness emanating from her classmates, and she knew for the first time since she had enrolled that there was hope. Maybe I'll survive this move to New Mexico after all, she thought.

Grace straightened her shoulders and dared to glance at the students seated near her just as the door of the classroom opened, and Miss Phipps made an entrance. She looked straight at Grace, and the girl felt her heart jump with trepidation. Not that stupid lunch sack, she thought.

Miss Phipps whispered to Mrs. Ellis and then directed crisp words to Grace. "Come with me, please."

"Go ahead with Miss Phipps," Mrs. Ellis said gently. "I'll send your assignments home with Adele."

Grace walked to the door on numb legs. She knew she was scared, but she didn't really know why. Surely the lunch sack infraction wasn't that serious. She followed Miss Phipps out the classroom door and was surprised to see her father standing there in the hall with a worried look on his face.

"What is it, Dad?" she asked, but immediately knew it was her mother. Fear clutched her throat with tight fingers, and she could hardly breathe.

"We have to go to Albuquerque. Your mother became very ill this morning after you left for school. I took her down to the hospital, and Dr. Smith rushed her to Albuquerque. He wants us to follow as fast as we can. She isn't doing very well, Baby." Her father's words came out quietly, but the desperate look in his eyes told the whole story. He took her arm, and they headed down the hall to the outside door.

Grace was surprised that her legs would move, but she found herself walking swiftly by her father's side. As they approached the car, she mechanically noticed the year on the license plate, and the thought hit her with a sickening blow. It's April 15, 1935, and Mama may be dying. As she slid in the door her father held open, she said disgustedly, "And I waste time today making dandelion curls and diagraming sentences. Why did I ever have to come to this stupid school? Oh, Mama, Mama."

2

John Shockey passed the Tererro Store and the post office in a swirl of dust as he headed out of town. He made a sharp right hand turn to get on the road to Pecos and then gunned his new Studebaker. He glanced up at the mine on the mountain and muttered, "Thank God we're not in the middle of a change of shift." He knew the next crew would come on at three o'clock.

There was no traffic, so the car gained speed as it headed away from the mine and down Elk Mountain. Grace held her breath as they negotiated a sharp curve on the gravel road and roared down a steep decline. She didn't dare look out the window because she knew her side of the road dropped straight down toward the canyon. They navigated another sharp turn at the bottom of the mountain and drove along Willow Creek until they crossed a narrow bridge over the Pecos River and approached the entrance to Holy Ghost Canyon. "We'll run up to our cabin and get a change of clothes in case we have to stay in Albuquerque," John told his daughter.

As they started up Holy Ghost Road, Grace glanced at the white painted hospital on the right. She shuddered as she thought of her mother being in a big impersonal hospital in Albuquerque.

The cabin the Shockeys leased was about a mile up Holy Ghost Canyon. John had picked this site because it was close to the doctor and the hospital. It was also the most beautiful place he had ever seen, and he hoped the pure air and the sparkling creek and the virgin forest would have a positive effect on his frail wife's health. "A high altitude might work wonders for her lungs," the doctor in Texas had advised.

At first Maggie Shockey had felt rejuvenated in the pristine wilderness paradise. She took long walks among the spruce and pine trees and fished in the sassy little creek. The squirrels and chipmunks seemed like friends, and she laughed at the bossy blue jays who loudly protested the presence of these new Texas neighbors.

But high altitudes and mountains also mean long bitter winters. As the cold dragged on and Maggie was unable to get out in the fresh air, her skin lost its rosy glow and became white and pallid. Her cough worsened, and John knew they were all in trouble. He had hoped spring and warm weather would effect a cure. While he threw clothes into a small suitcase, he realized they had purposely kept themselves from facing the truth.

Grace and John piled back into the car and were soon flying down the road, the Pecos River following them to the lowlands as it danced and tumbled away from the mountains of its origin.

Leaving the town of Pecos, John headed toward Glorieta, winding through heavily wooded cedar and pinon covered hills. Santa Fe was not far away, and they drove past it with hardly a glance. Albuquerque was now about fifty miles farther. "In about an hour we'll be there," John said to the drawn-faced girl sitting by his side. Glancing at her, so young and vulnerable, his heart ached when he contemplated what this day might bring.

The dependable Studebaker took the worried twosome on a steady course toward the big city of Albuquerque, which lay on the other side of the Sandia Mountain Range. Trying to distract his anxious daughter, John asked half-heartedly, "How did school go today?" He really didn't expect a positive answer.

Grace blinked her eyes as if to bring herself back from the dark morass of impending dread into which she had fallen. "You know I hate school, Dad."

"Yes, you always have," John said with a resigned note in his voice. Then he smiled as he remembered taking her to school after her sixth birthday. Grace had thrown a temper tantrum and announced she would not stay. John could not stand seeing his little girl cry, so he told her, "I'll take you home, Baby. You don't have to stay. You can start school next year."

Next year rolled around, and the same thing happened, John remembered. Maggie shook her head at her husband who could transact a business deal and close it to his advantage any day of the week, but he couldn't say "no" to his daughter.

Grace was eight years old the next year, and Maggie had informed John she would take the girl to school this time. John knew he must have looked embarrassed as he said in a determined voice, "I'll take her, and she'll stay this time."

The scene at school had started out as a perfect rerun of the previous years when John had tried to enroll his reluctant student, but this time she didn't get her way. "You are eight years old, Baby, so you have to stay. I'm sorry, but that's the way it is."

"I hate you!" Grace had screamed, and John had hastily left, fighting back the tears. And he didn't win back his pouting daughter until a week later when he brought home a little pony. Then Grace quickly forgave her father.

The pony brought Grace the companionship she needed. She was a lonely child because her only brother was almost twenty years older. She had been born to middle aged parents who doted on her and spoiled her in every way. She seldom played with other children, and when a child did come to the farm to play, the visit usually ended up in a squabble. She didn't know how to share her many playthings, and she selfishly wanted to keep everything for herself. The pony became the friend she needed.

Nora was a patient little Shetland that carried Grace over the hot sands of the Texas cotton farm without complaint. A strong bond grew between the gentle animal and her mistress, and for the first time, Grace learned to think of another creature before herself. She brushed her little friend and fed her and told here all her secrets.

John overheard Grace talking about Miss Jones, her teacher, one day as she attempted to braid Nora's tail. "She is so bossy, Nora," Grace confided. "You have to do everything she tells you to do, or you are in big trouble." Grace shook her head dramatically at the thought of the corner to which she was often exiled.

"Grace, do you remember your first teacher, Miss Jones?" John suddenly asked his silent passenger.

"How could I forget her?" Grace answered distastefully. "She was a homely, skinny sour puss."

"But you learned very fast, and in one year she had you caught up to third grade work. So you made two grades in one year, thanks to Miss Jones. Remember?"

Grace nodded and shrugged. "So?"

"So you were always a good student after the start she gave you in school."

But I never liked school," Grace insisted. "If I had my way, I would have stayed home and ridden Nora and forgotten about school. I always hated being older than the other kids, too."

John smiled. He knew his daugher's words were true. "But I wanted my pretty little girl to grow up and know something, dear, even though she only wanted to know how to ride a horse." John reached over and patted Grace's hand that lay curled like a broken little white bird in her lap.

Grace clutched her father's big hand and turned to him with sad gray eyes. "You and Mama have been so good to me. I guess I've been pretty much a spoiled brat."

John put his hand back on the steering wheel. "You've brought your mother and me immeasurable joy. We love everything about you, even if you are spoiled." He gave her an apologetic smile and continued, "We hated to make you transfer to a new school your last year of high school. We knew it would be difficult for you, and we are proud of you for making the adjustment as well as you have."

Grace stared unseeingly out the windshield for a few minutes and then turned a serious face to her father. "You know, Dad, maybe I do like school a little bit. It was horrible at first. Most of the kids are Spanish, and I couldn't understand their English too well, and I sure couldn't understand the Spanish they speak the minute they leave the class room." Grace hesitated a moment and added, "And I'm sure they couldn't understand my English too well, either. They say I talk funny, and I'm sure I do sound different to them."

"But you have become friendly with Adele, haven't you?" John asked as he passed a truck loaded with logs.

"Well, Adele is a sweet girl, but we just don't have too much in common," Grace said slowly. Then she added with a smile, "Except being spoiled, I guess. Adele is an only child, and she gets to do whatever she wants, too."

"That could cause problems," John commented with a smile.

"Oh, she's easy to get along with," Grace assured her father. "I don't imagine she has ever fussed with anyone in her life."

"Are there any other girls you like now that you've been in this school for a while?" John asked.

"Well, there's Monte May, whose father runs the dairy," Grace answered. "She's shy, but we're starting to get acquainted. I think I'll like her all right. And then there is Fabiola whose father is a boss at the mine. I believe she's Spanish and French. She's very pretty and very smart. I think I'd like to be friends with her if she ever decides to be interested in me." Grace rolled her eyes expressively.

"This sounds encouraging," John remarked and then added to himself, very encouraging! She would never have anything to do with her classmates in Texas. Maybe she's going to do better here.

"Oh, and then there is Dora Ortiz. She's Spanish, but I think I like her. She has red hair and very light skin, so she must be just half Spanish. I know the Anglo kids don't play with the Spanish kids, but I think I will if I like them, and I do like Dora."

"That's good," John commented, and before thinking, he added, "Your mama will be happy to hear you are becoming better socially adjusted."

The mention of Mama brought both their thoughts back to reality. John looked at his watch. "We'll be there in thirty minutes," he said flatly. "Why don't you just rest a while."

Grace put her head back against the seat and closed her eyes. She had never asked God for anything, but now the words ran over and over in her head, God, don't let Mama die. God, don't let Mama die. God, please don't let Mama die.

Grace dozed off, but she was soon aware the car was slowing down. She opened her eyes and realized they were close to Albuquerque, and her father was taking an exit off the main road. She wondered if all this were a bad dream, and she wished fervently she would wake up any minute, and reality would be different. Her father drove down a tree-lined street of stucco houses, and suddenly he swerved as a black cat darted in front of their car. Oh no! Grace screamed silently. A black cat means bad luck, she thought, remembering she had heard older people voice this superstition.

Her father made a turn into a parking lot of a big building. "This is the Lovelace Hospital," he said tightly. "We'll go in and see how things are."

To Grace, the hospital would always be a dim memory of white walls, stairs, doors, whitely attired women, and a tired doctor in a rumpled suit. She would remember following the doctor to a room and seeing her mother lying there still and quiet. She looked as if she were asleep.

"I'm sorry," the doctor said. "We did all we could, Mr. Shockey."

Grace walked behind her father to her mother's bed. John lifted up one of the lifeless hands and cradled it. Then he laid the hand down gently and pulled Grace to his side. Holding her firmly around the waist, he whispered, "I'm sorry, Baby, she's gone."

"She's asleep, Dad." Grace spoke in a determined voice. "Can't you see, Dad? She's just asleep." She picked up her mother's hand and felt a strange limpness in the fingers that she knew so well. "Wake up, Mama," she demanded. "Dad and I are here to see you. It isn't polite to sleep when we come to visit you. Wake up, Mama!"

"Kiss your mama goodbye," John said softly to the dazed girl. "We must tell her goodbye."

John leaned over and embraced his still wife. He put his head down on her breast. Then he kissed the lips that were so dear to him. "Goodbye, my darling," came the tortured words.

Grace watched her father with stricken eyes. "Tell her goodbye," he repeated. He meant his words, she realized, like the time he told her to stay at school.

Reality was pushing itself into Grace's shocked being. She leaned over and kissed her mother's mouth which was still soft and warm. "You can't leave Dad and me. Don't you love us anymore? Wake up Mama!"

Finally she realized that her coaxing was in vain, and Grace collapsed, sobbing next to her mother's inert form.

"Let her cry it out," the doctor advised her father.

John put his head down next to his daughter's stricken body and sobbed too. "What will we do?" were his despairing words. "How can we live without you, Maggie?"

After a while John slowly got up and gently lifted his daughter. Grace clung to him as she whispered the words, "Mama, Mama. No, no."

John took Grace to a couch in the corner of the room, and they clung together until the sobs subsided. He wiped his daughter's face and said brokenly, "I've got to go and make some calls and arrangements. You stay here with your mama. Tell her all about your new friends. She needs to know you are happier in your new school."

"But Dad," Grace protested.

"Stay here with your mother. I'll be back soon. You'll always be glad you had one last visit with her." John spoke deliberately and walked with firm steps out of the room.

Grace sat for a minute silently staring at the quiet form on the bed. Then she slowly got up and stood beside her lifeless mother. Taking one soft hand, she said angrily, "It was that horrible black cat, Mama. He caused the whole thing. Oh Mama, why did he have to run in front of our car?"

3

Grace sat on a flat rock in the shade of spreading silver spruce branches and contemplated the drawing pad on her lap. She studied her work and then squinted her eyes thoughtfully as she looked at a horse standing a few yards away from her in a fenced meadow.

"Drat," the frustrated artist muttered. "I don't have the withers right. Why don't you stand still, Dutch?"

On hearing her name, the black horse raised her head, whinnied softly, and started to trot away. "A lot of help you are!" Grace shouted at the retreating horse's tail. "If you would stand still a little while, maybe I could draw a decent horse picture." With a frustrated groan, she threw the pad and pencil in the grass. Then she got up from the rock and stretched her lithe young body toward the sky before falling in a heap on the ground, pillowing her head in her hands, stretching out her long legs, and gazing up at the expanse of blue overhead. She heard the creek murmuring as it went on its way down the canyon to join its big sister, the Pecos. She was aware of the leaves of the aspen trees whispering their quiet secrets to the unresponsive firs.

Grace lay for several minutes unmoving and relaxing. "Oh, it's so good to be home," she said out loud.

Then her mind went its own way, dredging up hurtful memories of the last two months. A picture emerged of the dusty cemetery which lay just outside of the town of Ira, Texas, where they had taken her mother for her final resting place. She remembered standing between her father and brother as the dull sandy clods of dirt were shoveled into the gaping hole. "They can't do that!" the stricken girl screamed. "Mama would never want to be there in that prison in the ground. Dad, Bruce, do something!"

The hysterical girl was led blindly away from the gravesite to the car and taken back to the farm house. Bruce's wife, Susie, tried to quiet and comfort her brother's broken little sister.

The words that finally caught the attention of the wounded girl were, "Your mama is in heaven, Grace, where she is all right again. She doesn't hurt anymore. She doesn't cough anymore. She's a golden haired angel with God. God needed her more than we do."

The crying ceased and Grace turned her teary eyes, now blazing with rebellion, to her sister-in-law. "I need her, Susie. She's my mother, and I need her. Don't ever say I don't need her."

"Of course you do. We all need her. But God probably has a job only your mother can do. You know the way she was, Grace. She could do so many things. She could cook the best food in the world, and she could sew the prettiest dresses, but she could do even more than that. She could dance like a ballerina, and she could sing like a nightingale. She reminded me of a beautiful princess who spread magic everywhere she went. She could always make people feel good after something made them feel very bad. I think she was really an angel God let come down to earth for a short time, so she could help us all here for a while. But now he needs her back in heaven."

Grace swallowed her sobs and asked, "Does she really feel good now? She isn't sick and isn't coughing anymore?"

"I'm very sure of that, darlin'," Susie assured her. "Keep that thought in your head when you start wishing she were back here. You don't want her to suffer anymore, I'm sure."

Grace settled down after the meaning of those words sank in. She knew she never again wanted to see her mother cough until she vomited blood. But she also hated that empty feeling in her heart, and she knew it would never go away. "How can I live without my mother?" she had agonized.

Susie is a good person, Grace thought as she lay resting under the tree, swiping at the tears with her sleeve as they crept down her cheeks. Bruce waited a long time to take a wife; but now he seems to have found the perfect woman, she concluded.

John Shockey and Grace had discussed staying in Texas on the farm. Bruce and Susie assured them there was enough room for all the family, and although her father seemed to want to stay, Grace knew she preferred to go back to the mountains. She would never be happy in the hot sandy plains again. She wanted to see pine trees, not mesquite bushes. She wanted to listen to the singing waters of Holy Ghost Creek and the Pecos River. They would take the place of her mother's sweet soprano melodies. She felt in her heart she had to return to Tererro.

There had been only about six weeks of school left after the funeral, and Grace proudly graduated with her class. For the first time in her life, a group of young people had suddenly become special to her. They all rallied around in her grief and offered support in her sorrow. Adele was her rock, shielding her from all difficulties. Monte May buzzed around in her thoughtful way, letting her know she wanted to be a good friend. "You can visit me this summer," she said, "and my mother will help you with any problems you have." The words of the compassionate girl made her feel good, but they also cut like a knife, for they made her realize anew that her own mother would no longer be there for her in the future.

Even the regal Fabiola let Grace know she felt concern. She gave her a beautiful silver bracelet her mother had bought in Paris. When Grace protested that she couldn't keep such an expensive gift, Fabiola airily shook her head and said, "I have others. Of course, you can keep it. My mother would be insulted if you refused it."

And so would you, Grace realized. So she kept the gift, and it became almost like a sympathetic friend as she wore it and touched it often to remind herself of the special giver. She held her arm up above her head, and the rays of the sun caught the silver in the bracelet and made it shine like diamonds. So beautiful, Grace thought, just like Fabiola.

Grace didn't realize she was now thinking of other people in the world besides herself. A whole new facet of her personality was developing as a result of her heartbreak.

The boys in her class had also added their support. They smiled at her from a distance, and she felt their tentative concern. Ramon still played tricks on her and smiled his cute little crooked grin.

"Welcome back, Tex," he said the first day she had walked back into class. "Where's your horse, Tex?"

Grace had looked at him with exasperation and said proudly, "Actually, she's in the pasture behind my house, funny boy. We brought her back from the farm."

"Oh? What's her name? Merrylegs?" Ramon's dark eyes danced at the thought of Grace and her long legs on a little pony.

Grace pursed her lips and said, "Her name is Duchess, for your information, and she is a beautiful black quarter horse. And she's fast. I'll challenge anyone to a race any time."

Ramon widened his eyes in mock admiration and became a rodeo announcer. "Make way for Tex, the Texas cowgirl, on her be-e-u-ti-ful racehorse, Dutch, the Flying Dutchman. Excuse me, ladies and gentlemen. I should have said, Dutch, the Flying Duchess."

Grace revisited this scene with Ramon and smiled in spite of herself. "He's such a rascal," she murmured out loud.

After a few minutes Grace sat up and looked at her Flying Duchess horse. I'm so glad Dad and Bruce decided I should have my horse here, she thought. And I hope someday I can show Ramon how fast my sweetheart can run.

Duchess whinnied again and started walking back to the fence toward Grace. Grace looked in the direction her head pointed and saw a rider coming down the road. So that's who you are showing off for, Grace thought as she watched a pretty sorrel stepping high toward them with a black hatted rider swaying easily in the saddle.

Grace smiled at the rider when he got closer. He and his horse made a picture she would like to paint. Handsome horse, handsome rider, she thought.

The rider turned his horse off the road toward the tree where Grace was sitting. "Hi there," he called in a friendly voice. "Brandy here wants to say hello to your horse." He pulled his mount up a few feet from the fence and rested his arms over the pommel of his saddle. "Hello, ma'am. I'm Jimmy Kirkwood. I like the looks of your horse. I don't think I've seen you before." His eyes scanned the girl reclining in the grass with unabashed interest. He took in the windblown dark hair and the smokey gray eyes gazing up at him through long black lashes. "I'm quite sure I haven't seen you before, and I sure never expected to lay eyes on anything as pretty as you in the canyon today. I just rode up here from Indian Creek to give my horse a little exercise. Do you live here?"

"Yes, I do," Grace said firmly. "I've lived here for several months."

"Well, I haven't ridden up here for several months. Does your dad work in the mine?" Jimmy asked with friendly curiosity.

"No, we have a farm in Texas. We came up here hoping the mountain air would be good for my mother."

"Oh, and was it?" Jimmy looked keenly into the eyes that were hypnotizing him.

"No," Grace answered as quick tears filled her eyes.

Jimmy immediately regretted his question. "I shouldn't have asked that. Forgive me." He patted his horse's neck and looked embarrassed.

"It's all right," Grace said as she lifted her hand for a quick brush at her eyes. "It happened about two months ago, but the tears still come when I least expect them."

"I know," Jimmy said quietly. "My mother is gone, too, as well as my father. The tears still happen to me, too."

"I'm so sorry." The words came out impulsively. He's lost both his parents, and he's not crying, she rebuked herself.

Jimmy slipped off his horse with a light step and tied him to a fence pole where the two horses nuzzled. "I think they like each other," Jimmy said as he walked over and looked down at Grace.

"Duchess is lonesome for another horse," Grace said. "She's used to being in the pasture with our other horses in Texas."

Jimmy settled easily down on his haunches and looked at Grace with concern in his warm brown eyes. "Is her little mistress lonesome, too?"

Sudden impatience surged through Grace. Who does he think he is to ask me questions like that? she fumed to herself.

Jimmy sensed the girl's unease and said quickly, "I don't mean to sound too personal. You just have kind of a lost look on that pretty face of yours." He hesitated a moment, and as he looked compassionately at Grace, she felt her chagrin vanishing.

"I guess it's my turn to be sorry," she said quietly. "You'll just have to excuse my manners today. I'm not thinking too straight. My name is Grace Shockey. We leased that cabin by the road and moved up here last fall. The doctor thought the climate might be good for my mother. We left my brother managing our farm. Mama felt better at first, but she started failing in the winter, and she died in April. We took her back to Texas to bury her, but we came back here for me to finish school. We may go back to Texas when the summer is over."

"If you can leave the magic of the Pecos River Valley," Jimmy said as he gave her a mysterious smile. "I came here to work in the mine three years ago. I told myself I would work for a short time and then go on some place else. Well, I'm still here. I bought a little land and a cabin up Indian Creek, and I don't think anyone could tear me out of here with a stick of dynamite. Do you know what I'm talking about?"

Grace glanced at the genial young man crouched beside her. She liked his dark hair that fell carelessly over his lively brown eyes and the strong white teeth that complemented his tanned good looks. She knew what he meant; she knew exactly what he meant.

Jimmy looked over at the horses and changed the subject. "Can your horse run?" he asked.

"Of course, she can run," Grace answered quickly.

"Maybe in Texas in that low altitude," Jimmy said with a smile. "I betcha she can't touch my horse in these mountains."

"Is that a challenge?" Grace asked slowly, her full lower lip jutting out.

"Call it what you want," Jimmy responded, putting a strand of grass in his mouth. "Brandy has never been beat in the Pecos Valley."

"Duchess can take him," Grace said evenly.

Jimmy stared at Grace for a long minute. She no longer looked like a sad little girl. As she stood up and loomed over him, tall and sure of herself, he thought, I found me a mountain goddess today. Then he stood and looked down at her with an amused smile tugging at the corners of his mouth. He took off his hat and said, "Well, it's truly my pleasure to meet you today, Grace Shockey. We'll have that race someday and settle this question. Right now I've got to head back to Indian Creek. I have to go to work on the evening shift. I changed from days to evenings today, so I had some extra time to take a ride." He put his hat back on and pushed it jauntily down over one eye. With a slight wink he went to the fence to untie his horse. Stepping lithely up into the saddle, he grinned and drawled, "See y'all again, Tex."

Drat! Grace thought as she watched him ride off. Why does everyone call me Tex? But she was smiling as she picked up her drawing pad and headed for the cabin.

John Shockey was sitting at the wooden table holding a cup of coffee and staring with dull eyes into space when Grace opened the door.

He had been quiet and withdrawn since their return to the canyon. He's just not getting over Mama not being here, Grace thought as she walked into the room.

She put her pencil and pad down on the table and suddenly had an idea. "Dad, let's do something interesting today. Let's go explore Indian Cave. I feel like getting away from the cabin."

John looked up at Grace with resignation and said with a sigh, "Whatever you want to do, Baby."

"Well, get any supplies we'll need—rope, flashlights, candles, I suppose, and let's go exploring. I'll fix us some sandwiches."

John got up mechanically and started putting things together. Grace took peanut butter and jelly out of the pantry to make sandwiches. I've got to get him out of the house, she thought. He can't sit here and think of Mama all the time. And she was in just the mood to get away from the cabin for a while since her encounter with Jimmy Kirkwood. I think he gave me some of that exciting energy he and his big horse have, she told herself with a smile. And I won't be challenging that horse to anymore races. I think he may just beat Duchess, she acknowledged with a rueful toss of her head.

4

"Do you think Indians ever lived in the cave, Dad?" Grace asked as she and her father drove down the Holy Ghost Road.

"Maybe, many many years ago, and from the talk I've heard, Indians have been known to make pilgrimages to the cave, probably to practice their religious rituals. But there have been no reports of their having been there for the past few years."

"I wish they would come back now," Grace said with excitement in her voice.

John looked at his young daughter and thought, I'm sure you do. You are never happier than when you think you're involved in an adventure.

John turned north on the Pecos Road and headed across the bridge. "I would like to get some fishing in today," he said. "I brought my fishing gear, just in case we have some time after our cave exploration."

Grace smiled at her father's plans. She was glad he was showing interest in doing something besides sitting in the house grieving.

Before John turned off on the side road which took them up to the cleft in the mountain, Grace said, "Dad, I have a good idea. Let's stop at the Owens' house and see if Monte May wants to go with us. I haven't seen her since graduation, and she would be a fun person to have with us today."

"Sounds fine to me," John said. It was gratifying to him to have his daughter showing interest in socializing with someone her age.

Cora Owens straightened up from her flower bed as the car came to a stop in front of the house. She waved and smiled.

Grace jumped out of the car and ran up to Mrs. Owens, who greeted her with a warm hug. For a moment Grace wanted to stay in her arms forever. She missed her mother's hugs. "We're going to Indian Cave to explore," she said breathlessly. "Do you think Monte May would like to go with us?"

"Why don't you ask her?" replied Mrs. Owens.

Monte May had heard their voices and had come to the door. Her round blue eyes and corn colored hair framed a questioning face. "Gracie! What are you doing here?" she said as she bounded down the steps.

"My father is taking me to the cave, and I wondered if you would like to go along?" Grace and Monte May stood staring at each other with unabashed pleasure.

Suddenly Monte May frowned. "I don't know about going into that cave."

"Don't be a scaredy-cat, girl. Of course, you know you'd like to go." Grace stared at her friend with impatience.

"Well, do you have lights? A person shouldn't go in there without lights," Monte May said.

"Oh yes," John Shockey assured her. "We have two flashlights and some candles. Come on. I promise to take good care of you girls. We'll have lunch at the mouth of the cave, so we'll be well fortified for our exploration."

Monte May looked uneasily into his eyes for a long moment. His steady gaze reassured her, and she said slowly, "Sure, I'll go with you."

Mrs. Owens smiled. "Go in and get a jacket and some of the ginger cookies I just baked."

As the girls disappeared into the house, Mrs. Owens said, "I'm glad she's going. Her brothers have been there several times, but they have never been able to talk her into going with them. This is a challenge for her, and I'm pleased she's taking it. Thank you for asking her."

"It's our pleasure," John replied. "Grace needs to get out and be with girls her own age. She can't stay at home moping all the time."

"I understand what you mean." Mrs. Owens nodded her head thoughtfully. In a moment she smiled. "We'll have supper about 6:30. Plan to eat with us."

John grinned his acceptance as the girls came running down the porch steps and hopped into the back seat of the car, all chatter and giggles. Mrs. Owens waved goodbye when the car moved out of the yard.

John parked as close as he could to the cave, and they climbed the rest of the way up to the entrance. They sat down near the entrance and unwrapped their sandwiches, taking large hungry bites and washing them down with rich milk.

"This milk came from your dairy," Grace said as she refilled her father's cup. "I love this milk, especially in the winter time when the cap has been pushed up by the frozen ice slivers. It's so delicious."

"Yes," Grace's father laughed. "She always makes sure she gets the first glass of milk because it's full of cream and ice. It's her own special ice milk shake."

"But these ginger cookies make it even better," Grace said as she dipped a brown sugary bite in her cup. "You'll have to teach me how to make these, Monte May. They are luscious!"

"Maybe you can stay overnight sometime, and I'll show you," Monte May said. "They are very easy."

"That would be nice," John commented. "Then you can make cookies for me instead of drawing horse pictures."

"Be realistic, Dad," Grace admonished. "You know that isn't going to happen."

"I suppose not," John Shockey sighed in mock resignation. "Well, come on, girls. Let's get going. You two take the flashlights, and I'll carry this big candle."

They slowly entered the cave where blackness soon engulfed them. Finally, they were following the streams of light, surrounded on every side by impenetrable darkness.

"Are you all right, girls?" John asked as he led them forward.

"Fine," came Grace's strong reply.

"Okay," was Monte May's weaker answer.

"Just keep close to me," John said.

They walked silently as their lights probed the darkness. When their eyes adjusted to the new environment, they could vaguely make out uneven rock walls where shadows eerily danced as their lights flitted over them.

Suddenly they came to a point where one part of the passageway veered sharply to the right. "We'll put the candle on this rocky ledge," John said. "Then let's sit down and just enjoy this cave for a while."

"I'm ready," Monte May announced as she found a rock. Grace and her father sat close by.

The girls ran their flashlights up and down the walls and to the top of the cave. "What is that little black thing up on the ceiling?" Monte May asked with a catch in her voice.

"That's a bat," John answered. "There are probably many of them in here. They sleep in the cave during the daytime and fly out at night to look for food."

"Do they bite people?" Monte May asked in a whisper.

"No," John answered quickly. "They are really friends to mankind. They eat pesky insects and harmful rodents. You won't see a mouse in here, I guarantee you."

"Thank goodness," Monte May said in a louder voice.

Grace had been cautiously looking around. "Do you think this cave might be a good home for animals, Dad?"

"Well, I imagine it would be a perfect home for a bear in the winter. And smaller animals might live here, too. There's room for a whole community, I would guess. That's why we aren't going any further."

John got up and the girls followed suit. As he reached for his candle, Grace stopped him. "Why don't you leave the candle here, Dad? Then maybe someone else can sit and enjoy the cave like we did."

"Good idea," John agreed. "I'll also leave these wooden kitchen matches here. Turn on your flashlights, girls. I'll blow this candle out and set it up on the ledge."

"If we ever come back, we'll see if our candle is still here," Grace said. "So, Monte May, we have to return to this cave some day."

"Let's get out first before we talk about returning," Monte May said in a breathy voice.

The distance back to the entrance seemed shorter than the way in. They spotted the tiny light at the end beckoning them back to the outside world, and they hastened their steps and were soon out in the bright sunshine.

Monte May shook her head trying to get her eyes adjusted to the change of light. "I did it! I did it! My brothers will never believe I really went into the cave."

"Well, we'll vouch for you," John said with a smile. "You did a good job and were very brave."

"Don't you ever call me a scaredy-cat again," Monte May laughingly said as she shook her finger in Grace's face.

Grace smilingly agreed.

"Girls, let's not linger," John said. "I want to get down to the bridge and cast my fishing line in a special hole there."

As John settled down at his favorite trout habitat, Grace and Monte May sauntered down the river bank talking and giggling.

"I'm going to school in Albuquerque this fall," Monte May told Grace after they had recalled and laughed over a few high school escapades.

"Oh?" Grace said, finding herself at a loss for words. She suddenly realized that she had no plans for future schooling. I don't want any more school, she thought decisively.

"Yes," Monte May continued. "Skipper Cooper is going to the university, and he wants me to go to school in Albuquerque, too. I'll be going to the Sandia Business School."

"Oh," Grace said again. She puzzled over the fact that Monte May and Skipper must have been more than good friends in high school. "Do you and Skipper have serious plans for the future?" she blurted out.

Monte May blushed. "W-well, we have plans for someday. Don't you think Skipper is a pretty swell guy?"

"I guess," Grace answered. I've never thought of Skipper one way or another, she thought. He's just a boy in my graduating class.

Monte May stared curiously at Grace. "Don't you even want a boyfriend?"

"No," Grace said instantly.

"Don't you ever see someone who looks kind of interesting, and you would like to know more about him?" Monte May persisted.

"No," Grace said again, quickly slipping out of her sandals. "Let's wade."

"I'm sure the water is awfully cold," Monte May objected.

"The water is fine," Grace announced, stepping in. "Come on in." As her friend hesitated, she added, "Remember, you're not a scaredy-cat anymore. Besides, it's going to rain on you if you don't." Grace splashed water in Monte May's direction.

"I'm coming!" her exasperated friend yelled as Grace started to splash her again.

The girls waded on the round pebbles in the shallow pool at the river's edge, "I see little fish in here. I'm getting out," Monte May said suddenly.

"They're just baby fish," Grace said. "They won't bite your toes."

"I'm getting out," Monte May repeated. She quietly sat on a rock and turned her cold feet to the sun.

"Oh, all right," Grace said as she waded back to the shore. "This warm rock does feel good under my feet."

The girls sat silently for a few moments. "To tell the truth," Grace said suddenly, "I guess there really is one fellow I met who kind of interests me."

"Who is it? Tell me about him!" Monte May said excitedly.

"Well, I actually saw him just today up the canyon. He rides a beautiful sorrel horse. He's not a boy like Skipper. He's older than me, but not much. You know, I'm nineteen years old now. He's a miner and a cowboy, I guess."

Grace paused, and it was Monte May's turn to say, "Oh?" and find herself at a loss for words.

"He's tall, dark, and handsome, as the saying goes, and has brown eyes and dark uncooperative hair. He wears a cowboy hat and pretty western boots."

Monte May looked unimpressed.

"He has a pretty smile, and he's nice," Grace added. "I know because I was feeling kind of sad, and he noticed it and tried to make me feel better." Monte May's expression warmed.

"Oh, that's good," she said. "I hope you're right, and he is nice."

Grace now felt embarrassed about her confession. She immediately wished she hadn't said anything about Jimmy Kirkwood. Grabbing her sandals, she said abruptly, "We'd better go back where Dad is. He's probably wondering where we are."

The girls quickly put their shoes on and ran up the river bank. John was just putting his gear in the car.

"Did you catch anything?" Grace asked.

"No," John said dourly. "But I had one, a big one. One about this big," and he stretched his hands out about sixteen inches. "I had him out on the bank, too, but he flopped around and got off the hook and flipped himself right back into the river."

"Oh Dad," Grace said with concern. "I'm sorry I didn't stay with you. I would have grabbed that fish and held on to him!"

John smiled over at his daughter. He knew she would have done just that. "It's all right," he assured her. "I'll come back and get him next time. Hop in the car now. We've got to head back to that good supper that's waiting for us."

When they arrived, John and the girls walked around to the back porch to wash their hands before going into the kitchen. Mrs. Owens was just setting the table. "Go on in the living room, John. You girls stay here and help me get supper on," she instructed.

Henry Owens and John Shockey easily launched into conversation and talked of their lives before coming to Tererro. Henry told John he could see the need of a dairy when he came to the bustling mining town, so he continued the work he had done all his life in Nebraska. "I love it here," he said. "I'll never leave these mountains."

"I like it here, too," John agreed. "But we'll probably go back to Texas in September. That's when our lease is up on our cabin. My son, Bruce, could use some help on the cotton farm."

"We'll hate to lose you," Henry said.

At that moment Cora called, "Supper is ready."

Everyone sat down to a round oak table with bowls of stew set at each place. A huge platter of hot biscuits dominated the center of the table, framed by freshly churned butter and raspberry jam. There was also a tempting wilted lettuce salad. Just like Mama made, Grace thought. She looked over at her dad and knew he was thinking the same thing.

But there was no time for melancholy thoughts as the group began their tasty meal. The conversation was as satisfying as the food. Being here is good for the soul as well as the body, John thought while he enjoyed hearty bites of vegetables and meat.

Dessert was banana pudding served with a ginger cookie. "I feel like I've died and gone to Food Heaven," Grace commented.

After dinner the girls stayed in the kitchen to do the clean-up chores. John and Henry retired to the living room to enjoy their pipes, and Cora sat in her rocking chair with her tired feet on a soft foot stool. "You have a lovely daughter, John. Feel free to call on me if you need help with her at any time. She's a good girl, but girls all occasionally need a mother's guidance at her age."

"I know, and I thank you, Cora. Sometimes it scares me when I see what a beautiful young woman she's becoming. She hardly knows young men exist yet, but I'm sure she will discover them soon."

"They will make her discover them," Cora said dryly.

The girls came into the living room at that moment. "Dad, I hear there's a ball game tomorrow," Grace said. "Why don't we go?"

"I've heard Tererro has quite a team," John answered. "Perhaps we'll do just that. Where's the baseball field, Henry?"

"Up in the meadow past Gifford Town," Henry replied. "It should be a good game. Tererro hasn't lost a game yet this season, but they're playing Espanola tomorrow, and they have a good team."

"We'll try to be there," John said. "We'll hope to see you all there. Now Grace, we have imposed on these folks long enough. We must head up the canyon."

Warm thanks for the meal were rendered, and John and Grace started homeward. John put his hand over on his daughter's shoulder. "I think we can make the summer if we have the hope of a meal with the Owens family occasionally. Don't you agree?"

"I surely do," Grace replied enthusiastically. But more than food, she was thinking about the two Owens boys, Mike and Tommy, who had come in the kitchen after they had finished their milking chores. They were charming, blonde, laughing young men whose merry eyes appreciated the looks of their sister's friend. They were the ones who had suggested the ball game.

Grace knew it was an encouraging sign that her father was talking about getting out of the cabin and attending a ball game. She also knew it would be good to see Monte May's brothers again! But they don't hold a candle to Jimmy Kirkwood, she thought to herself as she compared their boyish faces to the rugged chiseled features of the cowboy. "Life is suddenly more interesting," she murmured softly and flashed a dazzling smile at her father when he looked at her inquiringly.

5

Grace's eyes sparkled with anticipation as her father parked the car under the shade of a pine tree at the edge of the baseball field. She had never been to a baseball game before, and she immediately felt the excitement in the air. Crowds milled around eating popcorn and drinking soda pop and beer; herds of children ran squealing through the spectators, elated by the activity and the chance for treats and goodies. A ball game in Tererro meant a good time for all.

Grace felt a timid touch on her arm and turned to see a smiling face prettily framed with a carefully combed page boy hairdo beaming at her. "Dora Ortiz!" she yelled above the noise of the crowd. "How are you? It's been so long. What are you doing, and how are you getting along?" She put her arms around the girl's shoulders and embraced her tightly.

"I'm fine," Dora said as Grace moved back when she noticed someone peering over Dora's shoulder.

"There's Ramon!" Grace exclaimed. "How's my old buddy?"

A grin lit the young man's face like a beacon. "I'm very good," he said, "but not as good as my sweet girl here." He put his arm around Dora's waist and pulled her possessively away from Grace.

"Aha, and what does this mean?" Grace asked as Dora snuggled into Ramon's arms. "Does it mean what I think it does?"

"If you think Dora is my girl and only mine, you are right," Ramon announced proudly. "Tell her, querida."

Dora looked at Grace self-consciously with her soft brown eyes. "Ramon and I, we will soon be married."

"She will soon be my wife, Tex. Did I do all right in my choice?"

"You did all right, but I don't know about Dora. She deserves the very best. I don't know if that is you, Senor Ramon." Grace looked at Ramon from under her eyelashes with a friendly challenge.

"Oh, he is the best, the very best," Dora hastened to assure her friend. "And he's so handsome, don't you think?" She looked up at her prospective husband adoringly.

"Well, maybe," Grace said slowly. "You're sure you don't want me to look around for someone better for you?"

"Oh no!" Dora said seriously. "He's wonderful, Grace. I tell you the truth."

Grace relaxed her stern look and smiled as she offered congratulations to the happy couple.

"I know he is, Dora. I was just teasing—the way he used to tease me, the rascal. I'm so happy for both of you. When will you be married?"

"Soon," Dora answered. "As soon as the priest in Saint Francis Church in Santa Fe can perform the ceremony. Ramon is going to the Army this fall so we want to be married before he leaves."

"Oh," Grace said soberly. "Where will you live while he's gone?"

"Here with my parents at first," Dora said happily. "I have a job at Dodson's Store, so I'll be working. Maybe later I'll get a better job in Santa Fe. We'll be saving money to buy a house when he comes back."

Suddenly a feeling of foreboding came over Grace. What if he doesn't come back? she thought. She had been hearing war rumblings lately in the radio news. "I wish you both much happiness," she said aloud. "You know you are two of my most favorite people."

John Shockey took Grace's arm at that moment and led her away. "I see the Owens family. Shall we go over and join them?" Grace let herself be led away as she waved goodbye to her friends. Sweet little Dora getting married. She couldn't imagine this scenario. She knew instinctively that it would not all be a bed of roses for the young couple with Ramon away in the Service. "Thank God there is no war going on—yet," she murmured.

But her sober thoughts of Dora and Ramon were soon forgotten when the Owens family greeted them and led them to seats in the grandstands.

"This should be an exciting game," John Shockey remarked, "if these Miners are as good as you say."

"This team is sponsored by the American Metal Company," Henry Owens explained. "The company pays their expenses when they travel around the state, and some of the mine workers built this nice ball park and the grandstands. Tererro takes its baseball seriously. You surely are going to see a good game. Our team should win, I think."

Monte May's little brother, Tommy, pushed in between Grace and his brother, Mike. "The Tererro Miners will win. You betcha!" he chimed in enthusiastically.

"If you say so," Grace said uncertainly as she gave Tommy a smile. Then, slowly she began to feel Tommy's excitement rising inside her as well.

"See the pitcher out there?" Mike asked as he joined in the conversation. "That's Jim Kirkwood, and oh boy, he's so good. They don't get many hits off him."

Grace's eyes followed Mike's pointing hand off to the side where a player was throwing hard balls to a teammate who was catching them and throwing them back. Her eyes were riveted on the long muscular legs of the pitcher as he drew back to throw. She had studied the muscled legs of horses when she drew them. What muscle tone, she thought. What incredibly athletic legs.

As her eyes moved up the body of the ball player, Grace took in the small waist, the broad chest, and the tousled dark hair that peeked out from under the baseball cap. Even from this distance she could see the determination etched in his face as he fired one hard ball after another to his catcher. Somehow he looked vaguely familiar, and she turned to Mike to ask, "What is the pitcher's name again?"

"Jim Kirkwood," Mike repeated, "the best pitcher on the Pecos."

Jim Kirkwood. Suddenly it hit her. Jimmy Kirkwood, the cowboy she had met on Holy Ghost Creek! Of course. The same long legs, the same dark hair. He just looks a little different in a baseball uniform and a baseball cap than he did in his blue jeans, boots, and cowboy hat.

Grace could hardly believe her good luck in already getting to see the intriguing cowboy she had just met. Putting her hand up to Monte May's ear she whispered, "That pitcher over there on the sidelines, that's my cowboy."

Monte May looked at her with wide unbelieving eyes as she slowly said, "Jim Kirkwood is your cowboy?"

"Yes, I'm sure he is," Grace answered. "He told me his name was Jimmy Kirkwood. I didn't recognize him at first, but as I look at him now, I'm sure he's the cowboy I met. He told me he's a miner."

"Well, maybe he's a miner and a cowboy, but he is also the ace pitcher for the ball team. This is all very interesting, Gracie."

"Yes, I think I'll enjoy this game more than I expected. Let's take a walk before the game starts. The popcorn stand happens to be near where he is warming up. Come on, Monte May!"

John Shockey gave Grace some money and urged her to be back by the time the game started. The girls walked over to the popcorn stand and waited while Grace watched the pitcher closely. Suddenly, a tall blonde girl walked by and yelled, "Good luck, Jim." The pitcher acknowledged the call with a two-fingered salute to the bill of his baseball cap, but kept his eye on the catcher as he prepared to throw the ball again.

Grace felt a moment of irritation as she watched the pretty girl walk away with a smug look on her face. Before she realized what she was doing, she yelled, "Go get 'em, Jimmy! Do it for Tex!"

Monte May was just reaching for two sacks of wonderful smelling popcorn when she heard Grace's yell and Jim's quick response as he stopped long enough to reply, "Just for you, Babe!"

Grace's face flushed a deep red as Monte May gasped, "You lucky girl."

Grace tried to keep from acting flustered as she reached for a bag of popcorn. "I told you I had met him. Didn't you believe me?"

"You said you met a cowboy. You didn't say you had met the star pitcher of the Miners' baseball team."

"Well, now we both know," Grace said with a giggle.

The girls walked back to their seats just as the game started. It was a long hard fought battle, but Tererro came out on top at the end, thanks mainly to the pitching of Jim Kirkwood.

Grace had sat in a trance through the whole game, hardly realizing what was going on. She only knew that her eyes were glued to the motions of the pitcher when he was in the game. He is so spectacular, she told herself as she watched him zing his pitches with grace and ease past the frustrated batters. At the triumphal end of the ninth inning, he took his cap off to the roaring crowd and held it high in the air. Then he pointed it with accuracy to the spot where Grace stood cheering and made a slight bow in her direction.

"Did you see that?" Monte May squealed with delight.

"What?" Grace asked with mock nonchalance, but her heart was beating so hard she was afraid she would die on the spot.

"Come on, let's go congratulate them," Monte May said as she hopped down from her seat.

Grace followed her friend onto the baseball field where the players were being mobbed and hugged by admiring fans. Suddenly, she felt a sense of shyness. Maybe it was only a coincidence that Jimmy had apparently responded to her before the game. And maybe he was really waving to the blonde girl just now.

When Grace and Monte May got near Jimmy, he was engulfed by such a crowd there was no way to get any closer to him. As they were jostled by the excited fans, Skipper Cooper suddenly pushed his way to Monte May's side. "Quite a game, huh? What a team we have!"

Grace noticed the happy flush that darkened Monte May's face as she looked up into Skipper's excited eyes. "It was a great game," she agreed. "Grace and I were going to congratulate Jim."

"You'll never get to him," Skipper said with a wave of his hand. "You can see him later. We're having all the players over to our house for a little victory celebration. Why don't you and Grace come over and meet everybody."

The girls looked at each other, half closed lashes hiding the excitement they felt at going to this party. "We'll ask our parents," Monte May quickly said. "If it's all right, they will drop us off."

"Tell them I'll take you home," Skipper shouted as he was being pushed away from the girls. "Hope to see you later."

The girls found their folks in the crowd and got permission. "I'll drop you off and visit with the Coopers," John Shockey decided. "I've been wanting to meet Ted Cooper."

"Be home by ten o'clock," Henry Owens said. "Nice people or not, you don't need to stay any longer than that. And make sure you're not late. I don't want to go looking for you."

"We'll be on time," Monte May hastily assured him. "I might as well ride with the Shockeys, and you won't have to go out of your way to take me there."

"They're all yours, John," Henry said as he and his family turned toward their car. Tommy and Mike looked a little disgruntled. The day wasn't ending as they had anticipated. They had hoped Grace would come home to spend the night with Monte May.

John drove his passengers down through Gifford and Rico Towns and then turned right on the road to Tererro. The Coopers lived on a hill just above the town. Ted Cooper was superintendent over the mine operations, and the company furnished him with a comfortable home.

Skipper's father met John and the girls at the door and ushered them into the living room. "The young people are in the back yard," Ted Cooper said. "Go on through the kitchen and find yourselves some food. Be nice to those ball players; we're really proud of them."

The mine superintendent invited John Shockey to sit down on the couch that faced a rustic rock fireplace in one wall. "Let me get you a drink, John, while we visit a while. Do you want a beer or ice tea?"

"I'll take tea, thank you," John replied. He was a Baptist from Texas, and he didn't drink beer.

Ted lifted an eyebrow at John's drink preference and went to the kitchen to get his tea. It wouldn't hurt him to drink a beer to celebrate Tererro's win, he grumbled to himself.

Ted watched the two girls go shyly out the back door to join the party. Skipper immediately approached Monte May, and to his surprise, he saw Jim Kirkwood take three long strides to Grace's side. Wonder where they got acquainted, he thought as he poured tea for Grace's father.

Grace looked deep into Jimmy Kirkwood's irresistible brown eyes. "Congratulations on your win," she said. "You didn't tell me you were a baseball player."

"Come over here under this pine tree, and I'll tell you all about it," Jimmy said as he pulled Grace away from the group. "There are a lot of things I need to tell you. Sit down and I'll get us some refreshments."

Grace eased down onto the lush grass and leaned back against a tree. Closing her eyes, she let her thoughts roam. I can't believe this is really me. Here I sit under a pine tree waiting for a handsome baseball player to bring me something to eat and drink. Two months ago I was a dumb little high school graduate; now I feel like Cleopatra, Queen of the Pecos, rather than the Nile.

Grace then slowly opened her eyes and looked around at the milling group of celebrants. The pretty blonde girl Grace had noticed earlier suddenly intercepted Jimmy as he started back to the pine tree with two plates of food and two bottles of pop. Grace's eyes flashed wide open as she concentrated on the pair. Jimmy smiled and talked to the girl briefly, then he excused himself and headed back to Grace. The same one who wished him luck at the game today, Grace sourly noted.

Jimmy handed Grace a plate piled high with meats, cheese, and a roll. Then he set the drinks and his plate down on the grass. "Thank you," Grace said sweetly. "Who's your friend?" The fire in her smokey eyes sent a warning to the ball player.

Jimmy looked honestly confused. "What friend?"

"The blonde who keeps chasing you around," Grace answered sarcastically.

Jimmy looked perplexed a moment longer, and then a big smile lightened his face. "You mean Colleen? The blonde I was just talking to?"

"Colleen who?" Grace asked sharply.

"Colleen Barns. Don't you think she's cute?" Jimmy took a big bite of his sandwich and fixed amused eyes on Grace.

"Well, excuse me! I didn't mean to interfere with you or anyone else." Grace stood up and reached for her plate.

Jimmy's big brown hand caught her smaller white one and held it firmly. "What's wrong with you?" He looked questioningly into her perturbed eyes. "There is no one else," Jimmy said quietly. "There's no one else but you, Tex, and I don't think there ever will be, tonight or evermore." Grace suddenly found herself in Jimmy's arms. As she looked up into warm brown eyes brimming with confidence, she felt her body go limp.

He's going to kiss me. I want him to kiss me, she realized.

"Grace, my pretty Texas girl," Jimmy said slowly and intensely, "I am tempted to kiss you, but I'm not going to. And no one would really hold it against me since I pitched such a good game today, but I'll never deliberately do anything that might displease you. Remember that. Now sit here and eat your supper with me and tell me what a great pitcher I am. Later you will dance with me and tell me what a great dancer I am. Because, Grace, with you I can be great at anything—even dancing."

Jimmy took his arms away from the stunned girl, and she almost fell back on the grass. She caught herself and sat back as bright red embarrassment flooded her face. Reaching for her plate, Grace stood up with finality. "I'll go and eat with Monte May and Skipper. Please excuse me."

As she flounced across the yard toward her friends, she thought, you'll never tell me what I will do or won't do, Jimmy Kirkwood.

But instead of sitting down, Grace put her plate on the table and walked straight to the house and into the kitchen. She glanced into the living room where her father and Ted Cooper were visiting. She walked in and stood by her father's chair. "Excuse me, Dad," she said, "I'm not feeling well, and I'd like to go home now."

John Shockey looked up into his daughter's flushed face and perceived something was wrong. He rose immediately and expressed his thanks to Ted Cooper for the hospitality and led Grace to the car.

Grace put her head back on the seat and closed her eyes as her father headed for the highway. "I'm sorry, Dad," she said between tight lips. "You seemed to be having a good visit, but I just couldn't stay any longer. I hope you understand."

"It's quite all right, dear," John said. "I hope it isn't anything serious."

"I don't think so," Grace said in an expressionless voice.

"Well, I did have a very interesting visit with Ted Cooper. He tells me they're short on help in the bookkeeping department. Since I have experience in doing the books for the farm, he asked if I would be interested in a job."

"What did you say?"

"I told him we would probably go back to Texas at the end of the summer. But, I'm pleased that he was impressed enough with me to offer me employment."

"No, Dad, we are not staying here," Grace said with vehemence. "I don't fit in here. Let's go back to Texas as soon as we can."

"Whatever you say, dear," John answered.

Grace sat on her side of the car with her eyes tightly closed and tried to cope with the contradictory emotions engulfing her. What are these feelings I have for Jimmy? I know I am very attracted to him, and I wanted him to kiss me. Yet I was very angry with him for the power I felt he had over me. I was in heaven with him, but I wanted to run away from him, too. Dear God, help me. I think I acted pretty dumb tonight. He'll never want to see me again, but I'll die if I don't see him.

The young girl grappled silently with perplexing emotions of frustrated confusion and unexplainable exhilaration.

6

The days that followed the party were dreary for Grace, and she moped around taking little interest in her usual activities. She rode dully along the mountain paths not noticing the wild flowers or the songs of the birds. Duchess seemed to sense her depression and walked sedately through the woods with no life in her steps.

Grace tried to fish, but she grew irritated when her line snagged in trees and shrubs along the creek. One day after several hang-ups, she gave an impatient jerk to the line, broke off the hook, and stamped fitfully into the cabin, promising herself she would never fish again.

But John Shockey was oblivious to Grace's feud with the creek and the brush. One afternoon when he was trying his luck in the Pecos, Grace felt especially bored and lonesome. She read for a while but found her interest wandering, so she finally put the book down and decided she would make a cake for her father. This was unusual for Grace, as she very seldom had domestic urges. But today in her frustration, she felt like creating something in the kitchen.

She flipped through her mother's recipe book and found directions for a pound cake that sounded easy. I'll open some of Mama's peach preserves for a topping, she thought, as she started mixing the ingredients. She even sang a little song as she stirred. "All in the merry month of May when the green buds were swelling; Sweet William came from a western state and courted Barbara Allen." But the singing suddenly stopped and Grace stepped back from her mixing bowl in exasperation. "Drat!" she said to the air. "We don't have enough flour for this cake."

She had only one scant cup of flour instead of the two cups the recipe specified. "Of course I didn't think to check if we have all the ingredients when I started the cake," she berated herself disgustedly.

Grace debated her dilemma briefly. She had her eggs and sugar and lard all mixed up, plus one cup of flour. What to do? "I wonder if there is any substitute I can use for flour," she said aloud as she checked the cupboards. "Well, there's cornmeal, but I don't think I want a cornmeal cake."

The stressed cook found nothing she thought would work in the cake until she spotted the breakfast cereals. "Maybe I could substitute cornflakes," she said out loud.

The cake smelled good as it cooked, and Grace washed her counters and swept up the cornflakes and flour that had spilled onto the floor. She continued her song as she worked, "O Mother, Mother, go make my bed. Go make it long and narrow. Sweet William died for pure, pure love, and I shall die for sorrow."

When the cake had cooked the necessary thirty minutes, Grace opened the oven. A wonderful smell greeted her nostrils, but her eyes beheld the strangest looking cake she'd ever seen. It was flat and cracked and looked nothing like the lightly browned sweet concoction it should have been. "Oh dear!" she moaned as she lifted it out and set in on pot holders on the counter to cool. She nervously walked the kitchen floor wondering what to do with this mess. Finally, she reasoned that since it smelled so good, maybe it could taste just as good.

Taking a knife out of the drawer, Grace cut a small square from a corner of the cake, scooped it out, and started to lift it to her mouth. But as she elevated the fork, the cake dissolved into crumbs that fell all over the floor. She looked at her empty fork with dismay and then down at the floor. Her patience snapped, and her temper flared. "Damn, damn, damn!" she exploded. She threw the fork down and stamped furiously on the white specks on the floor. "Just stay there!" she ordered. She kicked at the crumbs one last time and then collapsed into a kitchen chair with her head on the table. Sobs racked her body. "Oh, Mama, Mama," she cried. "I'm such a bad cook, and I've got such a bad temper. You would never talk so terrible. I'm sorry, Mama. I'm so sorry. Oh Mama, why did you have to go away?"

The stricken girl sobbed out her frustrations for several minutes. Finally she raised her head and got up and walked over to the cake. The pan was only warm now, so she picked it up and carried it out into the yard. She headed to the creek bank and threw it upside down on the ground. She pounded the bottom of the pan several times, and when she picked up the pan, her pound cake lay in perfect form on the grass. Amazingly, it looked better on the bottom than on the top. Suddenly her vexation was gone, and Grace looked up at a blue jay perched on a branch of a pine tree and began to laugh. The blue jay flew nervously away. Grace regained her composure and said, "I didn't mean to scare you, pretty bird. I brought you some cake. Don't you see? My cake is just for the birds!"

Grace started back to the house just as her father drove into the yard. He waved and got out of the car, showing off four trout. "See what I brought home for supper?" he said proudly. "Had a good fishing day."

Grace quickly hid the cake pan behind her and opened the door for the fisherman. "Something smells good!" he exclaimed as he walked into the cabin.

"Well, I baked you a cake," Grace said with a smile.

"Wonderful! We'll have fish for supper and cake for dessert."

"Not so fast, Dad. I threw the cake out to the birds."

"You did what?"

"I threw it out. We have no flour, Dad, and you can't bake a cake without flour. I tried, and it just didn't work."

"I'm sure it didn't," John said, as he threw back his head in amused laughter.

"It's not funny, Dad," Grace said seriously.

"I'm sorry, Baby," John said. Looking at her woeful face, he added, "Let's go out for supper tonight. I hear the Ponderosa Lodge has wonderful food. Let's give it a try. I'll put the fish in the cooler."

"Good idea, Dad. Did I ever tell you how much I respect your ideas?" Grace snuggled into the comforting arms of her father and felt her good humor returning.

John pushed his daughter back gently. "Wash your face and comb your hair, and let's celebrate! Ted Cooper was telling me that's the place to go for good food and a good time. I think they'll even have some music tonight."

Grace quickly stepped out of her stained clothes and put on a pretty full skirt and a frilly white blouse. Then she splashed her face with cold water from the wash basin and combed her dark hair straight back. She looked into the mirror over the washstand to view the finished product. Her cheeks were rosy from the cold water, her eyes sparkled with anticipation, and she took the tube of pink lipstick her father didn't know she had and put just enough on her lips to make them glow. Running her fingers through her hair, she pulled it forward slightly over one eye. As she smiled at her reflection, she told herself, "Looking pretty good there, girl! Greta has nothing on me tonight." She had heard her father speak of his admiration for Greta Garbo, the actress.

Grace waited while her father changed from a fisherman to a gentleman. He quickly washed his hands and splashed his face and hair with water. He then put on stylish looking tweed pants and a short sleeved summer shirt. When he combed back his thick gray hair, it fell into a natural wave over the right side of his forehead.

"Do I look good enough to escort a pretty girl to dinner?" he asked solemnly as they headed out the door.

"Dad, you are so handsome! I'll probably have to fight the women off to keep them away from you."

John sighed. "I'm sure you would. I know my girl is a fighter. But we are going to have fun tonight. Maybe the Coopers and Owenses will be there."

And maybe Jimmy will be there too, Grace thought, smiling.

🐦 🐦 🐦

The Ponderosa Lodge was about four miles down the Pecos Canyon from Holy Ghost Canyon. Tall ponderosa pine trees bordered the winding road. "They stand there like trusty sentinels watching over this mountain road," Grace said as they passed close to a big tree that had been scraped by vehicles a few too many times. "The bark on that one is pretty scarred."

"Yes, they are fantastic trees. They must be very old. They were probably here when inhabitants were living in Indian Cave."

Grace nodded absent-mindedly as she concentrated on the right side of the road where the entrance to Indian Creek was located. Jimmy had told her his cabin and land were only a short distance up the road, and she could just make out the cabin through the trees. She caught her breath at the thought of Jimmy being there.

The lodge was situated on the left side of the road among beautiful tall pines with the Pecos River flowing behind. It was a huge rustic log building housing the office, restaurant, and dance hall. Small log rental cabins dotted the surrounding meadow. "I've always noticed this place from the road as we pass by. I can't believe we are really going there," Grace said.

"Yes," her father agreed, "and we should have come sooner. This can be your overdue birthday celebration. We didn't feel much like celebrating on your actual birthday." Both were quiet as they remembered that her birthday had been right after they returned from the funeral. "I should have brought your mother here. She would have loved it, but..." Grace knew he was going to say, "she didn't feel like coming."

"She's watching over us today, and I know she's happy we're here," Grace said quietly.

John parked the car, and they walked down the rock path to the lodge. They went through a big wooden door and stood waiting to be seated as they looked around at the attractive room. Indian rugs and pottery decorated the log walls. A large moose head ruled over the entire dining area. "What a unique room," Grace said. "I love the southwest colors, so bright and alive."

"Just right for a girl like you," John said, smiling.

The waitress who came to seat them turned out to be Adele Johnson, whom Grace hadn't seen since graduation. "Hello, Adele," she said with surprised pleasure. "It's so good to see you. I didn't know you worked here."

"Yes, my mother got me the job. She works here cleanin' the cabins. I like it a lot."

Adele looked older and more sure of herself now. Her wild red hair was caught neatly in a hair net, and her uniform was clean and pressed. She looks so different, Grace thought.

"Do you want to sit in the back whar you can look out at the river?" Adele asked.

"That would be perfect," John said graciously.

After they had ordered, Grace looked out of the window. "The Pecos must be the most beautiful river in the world," she felt compelled to say.

"Well, yes. It heads not too many miles up in the mountains above Cowles. It's pure mountain water here. It hasn't had time to get muddy and dirty."

"Well, I'm glad I live here where it's clear and sparkling," Grace said. After a pause she continued, "Dad, I said I wanted to leave here. I'm not so sure now. How could I ever leave Tererro and all this beauty?" she said, pointing to the river rippling and splashing outside the window.

"I've been thinking along those same lines," her father replied. "The Texas Plains don't sound that great when I compare them to what we have here. Maybe Bruce can just keep running the farm, and you and I will stay here. Would you like that?"

"I think I would," Grace said thoughtfully. "I was out of sorts when I told you I wanted to leave."

John and Grace smiled at each other about their mutual decision. The tender roast beef, mashed potatoes, and gravy only added to their satisfaction. They were even more pleased when they noticed the Cooper family taking a seat at another table. "I'll talk to Ted Cooper tonight about a job," John said, a note of pleased determination in his voice.

Grace sat quietly for a few minutes as she considered her father's remark about getting a job. It suddenly occurred to her how many changes were going on with the people she knew. She thought of Dora and Ramon getting married, and Dora going to work, and Ramon joining the Service. Skipper and Monte May would be going to school in Albuquerque. Adele has a job already and obviously loves it. And what am I doing? she pondered. "Dad, do you think I should consider going to some kind of a school? What shall I do? I've got to do something."

"It would suit me if you just stayed home and were Daddy's little girl," John replied with a grin.

"Dad, you know that isn't realistic," Grace said seriously.

"Perhaps you're right," he said slowly. "We'll think more about this matter later. Tonight we're celebrating."

When the meal was over, the diners moved to the dance hall as the fiddlers tuned their instruments to the guitars. John took Grace out on the floor for the first dance, but other partners soon appeared and whirled her around the room. The tall dark haired girl with the graceful long legs was being noticed. "Where have you been hiding all my life?" was the constant question. Grace smiled and tossed back her long silky locks at each hopeful admirer.

The Owens boys came later and immediately took possession of Grace. She danced with one and then the other. They were energetic dancers and good company, but finally she sat down and begged for a little respite. "I must rest a few minutes."

Mike and Tommy went off to find other partners, and Grace made her escape to the back porch overlooking the river. She stood there quietly enjoying the sound of the musical water as she breathed the cool air. She felt happier with the world than she had for a long time. "What a lovely night," she murmured to herself, closing her eyes and savoring the magical beauty of the evening.

Suddenly, there was a soft touch on her shoulder. Grace turned around, and for a moment she didn't recognize the man who stood before her. He wore a hard hat with a light, and his work clothes were covered with spots of mud. He quickly removed the hat, and his thick unruly dark hair fell over his forehead. "Hi Tex," he said softly. "Don't you remember me—Jimmy Kirkwood?"

Grace's heart skipped a beat. "Of course," she gasped. "I just didn't recognize you in those clothes."

"I told you I was a miner," he said.

"Yes, of course. You are a cowboy and a miner and a pitcher. I remember that."

"I just stopped by on my way home to eat a bite. I took a shower in the Dry House, but I guess my clothes leave a little to be desired. I hope you'll excuse me. I'm glad to see you, because I have been thinking I should apologize for my behavior at the party. I'm sorry for the way I acted. You probably thought I was trying to get fresh."

Grace didn't quite know how to respond. She only knew she was glad to see him. Her voice seemed to have escaped her, and it was a few moments before she could respond. "I appreciate your concern for me," she said finally. "But I have to tell you something. Jimmy, I guess I'm kind of spoiled, and I have a bad temper. I don't like people telling me what to do, but I think I overreacted. And I guess I was kind of jealous, too. So, I'm sorry."

Jimmy smiled broadly. "An honest girl. How about that!" Then taking her hands gently in his, he said, "It would be hard not to spoil you if a person had a chance."

"That doesn't really excuse my temper," Grace said, looking up into his eyes.

Jimmy smiled. "You're one of those people who blows her top and then wants to make up in five minutes. Right?"

Words escaped her as she stared into the depths of his warm brown eyes.

"No harm done," Jimmy said softly, pulling her closer. "I wish you could see yourself with the river in the background. You look like a queen."

"Maybe I'm the Pecos Queen," Grace said lightly.

Just then the faint notes of "Over the Waves Waltz" wafted out onto the porch. "Dance one dance with me," Jimmy said softly. "We can't let the magic of this moment escape without one waltz."

Grace forgot all about his soiled work clothes as she opened her arms to him. It felt natural and right being held close and swaying to the music. The lilting river notes added tenderness to the fiddle melody as the two dancers melted together in perfect harmony.

After a few minutes Grace looked up and said dreamily, "You dance very well, Mr. Kirkwood."

"I'm inspired by my partner," Jimmy replied.

When the music came to an end, the two young people remained in an embrace neither one could bear to break. "Thank you," Jimmy said huskily. "Now may I dare ask to kiss the Pecos Queen?"

"You don't have to ask," Grace said as she lifted her lips to his. The river seemed to purr more contentedly, and the stars shone more magically as Grace drank in the sweetness of her first kiss. She instinctively knew she had been living all her life just for the touch of these lips on hers. She wanted this moment to last forever. "My little queen," Jimmy whispered, running his rough fingers through her silky hair.

Suddenly a voice broke the spell of the river and the stars. "Grace, it's time to go home," came her father's stern voice.

Jimmy instantly stepped back as John Shockey appeared out of the shadows. "Grace, who is this man?" he demanded.

"Jimmy Kirkwood," Grace said nervously. "Don't you remember? He's the pitcher for the Tererro baseball team."

John Shockey surveyed the miner's rough work clothes with distaste. "It's time for my daughter to go home," he barked impatiently.

"Of course, sir," Jimmy said evenly. "I also need to go home, clean up, and take care of my horses."

Jimmy picked up the hard hat he had dropped and quickly headed down the steps of the porch. "It was good to see you again, Grace. I hope to see you another time. Good night, Mr. Shockey."

"Good night," John replied coldly.

"Dad, you weren't very nice," Grace said as Jimmy vanished in the darkness.

"It's not appropriate for you to be out here kissing a stranger," John said pointedly as he escorted her down the steps toward the car.

"He's not a stranger," Grace replied.

"You barely know him," was her father's short response.

They drove silently through the shadows of the tall pines as they headed for home. "Why are you so unhappy with me, Dad?" Grace finally asked.

"I do not approve of your actions," John answered. "Your mother isn't here, and I feel it's important to take care of you the way she would have done. And she would not have been happy with your behavior tonight."

Later that night, Grace lay on her bed and looked out the window at the same stars that had sparkled down on her as she experienced her first kiss. She felt like a new person. The old depressed Grace was gone. Jimmy, I wonder if I am going to fall in love with you, she thought as she sighed dreamily.

7

The man who faced Grace the next morning was not the kind, patient father she had always known. John Shockey pounded the breakfast table and spoke in an emotionally charged voice.

"I will not have you messing around with a miner!" he shouted. "Do you understand me?"

Grace looked directly into her father's eyes. "I'm not 'messing around.' I don't know what you're talking about. I barely know Jimmy."

"That's exactly the point," the irate father roared. "You don't know him, and you will never know him. My daughter will not marry any miner."

"I don't plan on marrying anyone," Grace replied. "I'm too young."

"That's exactly right," John said, his red face turning a deeper shade of crimson. "You are too young, and you are too good for a miner, in plain language. Your mother came from one of the best families in Houston. She would be mortified if I let you become involved with a common miner."

John's rage was kindling a similar fire in his daughter. Grace felt hot resentment spreading over her whole body as she stood up. "Don't bring my mother into this. My mother always loved me, whatever I did. She would never let you treat me like this," she said through clenched teeth.

Moving swiftly toward her, John grabbed Grace by her shoulders. "I am your father, and you will do as I say. Mark that down, missy."

Grace quickly wrenched loose from his punishing hold, and tears streamed down her face. "Leave me alone," she sobbed as she ran to her bedroom and slammed the door loudly behind her. Her father stamped out of the house and roared down the road in the Studebaker.

Grace fell on her bed and curled up in a tight ball. Sobs shook her slim body, and the pain of the last months, plus this hurtful encounter with her father, engulfed her in a sea of agony. "Mama, Mama, Mama," she cried brokenly.

The tears finally ceased, but Grace lay there weak and spent, unable to move. "Let me die and be with you, Mama," she prayed.

Sleep must have finally overcome the emotionally exhausted young girl, and she woke with a start when she heard her father's voice at her bedroom door. "Get up and come in here. I want to talk to you." His voice sounded more normal now.

"What do you want?" she asked in a cautious voice.

"Come out, and I'll tell you."

Grace slowly entered the kitchen and looked at her father uncertainly. His eyes softened as he saw his daughter's hesitation. "Come and sit down. I won't hurt you," he said in a gentle voice.

Grace did as her father directed, and he dropped into a chair, covering his face with shaking hands. "I'm sorry, Grace," he said in a halting voice. For a moment his body trembled, and then he slowly placed his hands on the table. He looked at Grace with contrite eyes. "Baby, I'm totally responsible for your well-being. I only want to raise you in a way that would please your mother."

"She wouldn't want you treating me this way," Grace said dully.

"I said I'm sorry," John repeated, but let's talk about the other subject we mentioned last night. Perhaps some more schooling for you."

"You know I don't like school," Grace answered.

"I know that very well," her father replied. "But I may have something that will interest you. Neither one of us wants to go back to Texas, but we can't stay here and do nothing. Ted Cooper told me he has a place for me in the mine office, so that will take care of me. I go to work Monday."

Grace nodded. It didn't really matter to her what he did. Her emotions were so spent she felt like a spectator to this conversation.

"What if I found an art school some place?" John looked at his daughter with his old concern showing in his eyes. "I'm sure I could find a good art school back East for you."

"Back East?" Grace erupted. "I don't want to go back East!"

"All right," John said hastily. "Then I have another idea. Last night I met the woman who manages the Ponderosa Lodge, and I have just come from another conversation with her. She told me that an art school has been established in Santa Fe, and they plan to send a teacher to the lodge every day. The classes will run from nine to eleven in the mornings. I told Leota you might be interested in signing up. How does that sound?"

Grace's tired eyes sparked with interest at the prospect of taking a class in which she didn't have to do anything but draw. Slowly she asked, "You mean I could study art right there at the lodge?"

"That's what I'm saying," John replied. "Would you like that?"

"Dad, I would love that," Grace said quietly, her eyes brimming with tears. She wiped the back of her hand over her face to hide her emotion and said, "By the way, who is Leota?"

"Leota Stevenson, the manager of the lodge."

Grace was still struggling with tears, and John came around the table and laid his hands gently on the trembling girl's shoulders. Putting his finger under her chin and lifting her tear stained face, he said, "I'm afraid I don't always know what you would like. I'm just a dad, you know. But I thought you might be interested."

"I would love it," Grace asserted again in a firmer voice, jumping to her feet in excitement. "That's the kind of school I would like."

"Good. Now I want to mention something else to you. Sit down. We have more to discuss," John said, holding her chair for her. He then went around the table and sat down again. "This same woman, Leota Stevenson, also told me she's going to open a gift shop in conjunction with the art school. Students will have an outlet for the work they do. Of course, she will have other typical gift store items for sale like Indian jewelry and pottery. She's going to hire a part-time person to work in the gift shop. I asked her to consider you. How does that idea strike you?"

"Do you think I could do it?" Grace asked anxiously. "I've never had to do much work of any kind."

"Of course you could do it. You're a smart girl and can learn to do anything. You would go to art class in the mornings, and work in the gift shop in the afternoons and all day on Saturdays. That would keep you pretty busy; I hope not too busy. I'm going to be working, so you'll also have to get things done around the house when you're not on the job. Maybe you can watch them in the kitchen at the restaurant and learn to cook. Then when I come home from work, I won't have to worry about our meals."

Grace thought of her attempts at cooking and shrugged her shoulders. "Miracles do happen, I guess."

John jumped up from the table and said with renewed enthusiasm, "Wash your face and pretty yourself up, and I'll take you down to the lodge to talk with Mrs. Stevenson. Don't you think this is kind of exciting? My little girl is grown up enough to apply for a job!"

Grace stood up and returned his smile. "I'm more excited about the art class," she said. "It will be fun learning to do real art, and I'll enjoy meeting new people. As far as learning to cook and doing all the domestic chores at home, that just may not happen. I might as well be honest with you, Dad."

John knew this to be an honest statement. He was sure his headstrong talented daughter would always be happier drawing a picture than cooking and cleaning a house.

Grace dipped cold water into the washpan and splashed her face vigorously. She combed her tousled hair and faced her father with a smile. "Let's go," she said. "Grace Shockey is ready to start her career as an artist and a sales clerk. Look out, world!"

"Amen!" John said under his breath.

8

As they walked into the lodge, Grace was struck with the realization of how different it felt to come in as a prospective employee than as a patron. There was a little hesitation as well as pride when she quickly scanned the large dining room. Fresh clean tablecloths with a single wild rose in the middle of the tables, she noted. So pretty.

At that moment, a woman came out of the office and walked toward them. Her short auburn hair was swept back from her forehead in deep waves. Her lipsticked smile was warm and earthy over perfect teeth. High heels clicked sharply on the shiny hardwood floor, and her full skirt swung suggestively from hips which moved with a daring rhythm. The voluptuous curve of her breasts defied the prim high necked blouse gathered in at her trim waist with a silver and turquoise Indian belt.

"Hello John!" she said with obvious pleasure as she held out a white hand tipped with bright red nails. Silver bracelets jangled on her wrist and turquoise rings adorned her fingers.

"Hello Leota," John smilingly responded. "This is my daughter, Grace. Grace, Mrs. Stevenson."

Leota turned her large brown eyes to Grace, who suddenly felt young and uncomfortable. "You're here to talk about the gift shop job," she said. "John, you go have some coffee and a roll while we talk. The cook has wonderful cinnamon rolls today."

John flashed his daughter a smile of encouragement and headed for the counter at the other end of the room. Leota quickly wheeled and motioned for Grace to follow her into the office. Grace took the chair which Leota indicated as her prospective boss swished around her desk, leaving a sweet smelling fragrance of wild roses wafting in the air.

"Your father has told me something about you," Leota said as she reached for a folder on top of her desk. "You are nineteen years old, and you graduated from high school in Tererro. Right?"

"Yes, ma'am," Grace confirmed in a low voice.

"Don't be afraid of me, girl. I won't bite," she crisply dictated as she took a pencil in her right hand.

"No...yes...I mean," Grace stuttered. Then she lifted her chin and looked straight into the older woman's eyes. "I am not afraid of you, Mrs. Stevenson," she said in a firm voice.

"Call me Leota, please," the woman said, obviously slightly amused. "Let's talk about this job."

Fine, Grace thought. That's what I'm here for. And for all your painted and bejeweled finery, dear lady, you are not quite as impressive as you would like me to think. You are not going to intimidate me.

"These would be your duties," Leota said briskly as she pushed a sheet of paper across the desk. "You will be in charge of ordering, pricing, and selling the gift items we carry. I'll require you to keep a simple set of books on all sales and expenditures. Did you take accounting in high school?"

"Yes, ma'am."

"Were your grades good?"

For the first time in her life, Grace wished she could say yes. "I passed the course," she said quietly.

"Hm-m," Leota said. "Didn't like school that much, huh?"

"How did you know?" Grace asked in surprise.

Leota winked one of her warm brown eyes at the nervous girl. "Don't worry about it. I didn't like school myself."

"Oh," Grace said looking down. She had started to dislike this woman, but now she realized she would have to reserve judgment.

"I'm sure you learned enough to do what will be necessary to work in the shop," Leota said with a wave of her hand. "Now, I will expect you to help out occasionally in the dining room, perhaps even in the kitchen when we are having special affairs. I don't suppose you've had much experience in either of these areas?"

"No, ma'am," Grace answered, "but I will be happy to try."

"That's all I need," Leota said with a smile. "If you try hard, you'll learn to do these things. I will want you in the afternoons from one o'clock until six on weekdays and all day on Saturday. Sundays you'll have off. Depending on our schedule, I may need you to work a little later some evenings. Does this sound like too much work to you?" Leota looked at the girl with discerning eyes.

"I don't think so," Grace said quickly, realizing that the woman knew she had never worked before.

"Well, we'll try it for a while," Leota said. "It will be good for you, and we can certainly use the help."

Grace suddenly found herself elated with the idea that she had just gotten her first job. She smiled, and Leota thought, as she looked at the perfect heart face framed with dark silky hair and dominated by smokey gray eyes, she's gorgeous, and she doesn't even know it. A little class will be good for this place.

"Do you have any questions about the job?"

"No, ma'am."

"Well, you've forgotten a very important detail, my dear," Leota said, tapping the desk with long red fingernails. "Aren't you interested in the salary?"

"Oh, yes," Grace replied, feeling embarrassed. "I suppose I should find out about the salary." Grace nervously twisted a strand of hair.

"We'll start you out at ten dollars a week," Leota said swiftly, as if wanting to bring this interview to a close.

"Thank you very much," Grace said appreciatively. "I'll try my hardest to do a good job. When do you want me to begin?"

"Come down in the morning. Are you planning on signing up for the art class? Your father said you might be interested."

"Yes," Grace said enthusiastically. "I surely would like to take the art class."

"Then you can go to work tomorrow afternoon after the class. How does that sound?" Leota stood up and extended her hand.

"Wonderful!" Grace replied, as she took the hand of her new boss and squeezed it gratefully.

Leota then came around the desk. "Come with me, and you can meet the rest of the crew."

Grace hurried to keep up with the shapely legs walking ahead of her. She noticed her father sitting at the far end of the room and waved to him. He smiled and waved back.

Leota went through the dining room to the kitchen, where a stout Mexican woman was stirring a pot of steamy spicy food on a large black wood stove. "Angela, this is Grace. She will be working here at the lodge, starting tomorrow. Grace, this is our cook, Angela."

Grace took in the big pots on the stove from which tantalizing smells were steaming, the salad table covered with vegetables, and a large counter laden with fresh rolls, pies, and a big flat cake waiting to be frosted. Contrasted to the limited cooking that had gone on at home since her mother died, Grace was amazed at all the food. She smiled at the cook. "I'm so happy to meet you. Maybe you can teach me to cook some of this wonderful food. My father would like that."

Leota focused her eyes keenly on Grace, and the cook looked as if she didn't know what to say to this girl who had suddenly invaded her domain. Sensing she was serious, Angela said hesitantly, "I teach you, if you want."

Leota took Grace by the arm, and they went out of the kitchen and headed for the counter where John sat eating his roll. A waitress was standing nearby filling sugar containers. She turned as they sat down on a stool.

"Adele!" Grace said, recognizing her friend. "I'm going to work here. Isn't that fantastic?"

Adele's usually expressionless face broke into a pleased smile as Leota said dryly, "Well, you girls are obviously glad to be working together. But don't get too excited, Grace, until you see how much work you are going to have to do." Leota looked at John and winked.

Just then a woman in a white uniform came in the side door that led to the back porch. She sat down at the end of the counter without looking at the other occupants and addressed Adele, "I'll be a takin' my lunch break now. Bring me a egg sandwich."

Leota spoke over John's head to the woman. "Mrs. Johnson, this young lady is Grace, and she will be working here with us now. It seems she and your daughter are already good friends. Mrs. Johnson takes care of the cabins, Grace."

The cleaning lady raised her bleak eyes and barely acknowledged the new employee. Adele set a glass of water in front of her mother and said, "Mama, this here is Grace Shockey. You 'member me talkin' 'bout her from school, don'cha?"

Mrs. Johnson looked over at Grace with more interest. "O'course I 'member." A broad smile crossed her plain face.

"I'll be working here, Mrs. Johnson. Maybe I can help you, too," Grace said brightly.

Leota raised her perfectly penciled eyebrows and smiled at John.

"See, I told you she'd be a good worker," he said with a grin.

Grace caught the looks between John and Leota and thought, those two seem to have had quite a lot of conversation in the short time they've known each other.

Then Leota turned to Grace. "Young lady, all your time will be needed the first week to get that gift shop in order."

"Yes ma'am," Grace said quietly.

Adele brought her mother's sandwich and then asked Leota, "Is it all right if'n I take my break now? Grace and I could sit out on the back porch. I'll keep my eye on the dinin' room if'n a customer comes in."

"Surely," Leota said as she eased down on the stool next to John. Grace glanced back as she and Adele went out the door just in time to see Leota turn toward her father provocatively and cross her slim ankles. The sudden realization of the attraction this woman felt toward her father briefly surfaced, and for a moment she felt a flash of antagonism. But it was quickly forgotten as she and Adele sat down at a table on the porch and breathed in the sweet fresh Pecos River air.

Both girls beamed at each other for a few moments. "Isn't this just the best?" Grace said. "This is going to be so good, being with you every day. I've missed you, Adele."

"We'll be workin' most o' the time, you know," the practical Adele replied.

"But we'll see each other. It's been a lonely summer for me, Adele."

Adele looked apologetic. "I s'pose it was. I don't know what I'd do without my mama."

"You'd do just what I do—be lonely and miserable," Grace said. She leaned back in her chair and stared at the river as it moved musically along. Her mind went back to the night she and Jimmy had stood here in each other's arms. Suddenly she asked, "Adele, do you know Jimmy Kirkwood?"

"Sure," Adele replied. "He lives right over there 'cross the road and up Indian Creek a little ways. I've seen his house. You know, ours is down the road only a couple o' miles." Adele quickly looked downstream along the river. "Speak o' the devil," she exclaimed. "There's Jimmy now."

Grace's heart skipped a beat. "Where?"

"Right down there a ways. He often rides his horse when he ain't workin' day shift. He rides up this river trail a lot."

The girls sat quietly and watched the rider slowly approach. "Hi, Adele," he said. "I need a bottle of strawberry soda pretty bad." His eyes were fastened on Grace.

"I'll git you one," the waitress said as she vanished through the door.

Jimmy pulled up near the porch. "Hello, Tex," he said with a smile. "I thought I was dreaming. I was thinking of you being on the porch with me last night, and here you are in the flesh."

"Hello, Jimmy. I was thinking of you, too," Grace said breathlessly as she got up from her chair and eased over to the railing. "I'll walk with you for a short distance, if you don't mind."

About that time Adele came back and threw Jimmy the pop, and he tossed her a nickel. "Tell Dad I've gone for a walk down by the river," Grace said. And, with a wink she added, "Don't tell him who I'm with."

Adele nodded. "I wonder how she knows him," she muttered as she started back inside.

Jimmy and Grace were only a short distance down the trail when he reined in his horse and slipped down. "Let's sit on this rock and watch the river go by," he said. "I'll give you some of my soda."

"I can't stay long," Grace said quickly as she took a long sip. She watched the bubbles fizz to the top. "I love strawberry soda. It's so uplifting. It makes the worst day seem wonderful."

"It's a perfect day, now that I've seen you," Jimmy said as he pushed back the dark hair that hung over one eye. "I've been thinking about you. I hope you didn't get into too much trouble last night."

"Well, I did," Grace said flatly. "Dad was very disenchanted with me. He says I'm not to see you anymore."

"Why?" Jimmy asked as his face started to flush. "That can't be."

"Well, that's what he says, and he means it."

"What's wrong?" Jimmy said as he gripped Grace's arms and looked angrily into her eyes. "Why doesn't he like me? Is it because he thinks I'm not good enough for you?"

When Grace didn't answer, Jimmy dropped his arms. "That's it, isn't it? I'm not good enough for Daddy's little girl."

"I don't know what's wrong with him. Maybe he's not over losing Mama, and he doesn't want to think of sharing me. I just don't know, Jimmy. But I do know I want to see you again."

"You bet you do," Jimmy said. "And he's not going to stop us."

"Settle down, Jimbo," she said, placing her hands on his shoulders as she drew close to him. "Guess what? I got a job here today. I'm going to be working in the new gift shop Leota is opening. And I'm also going to be taking art lessons every morning." Grace ran her finger gently along the tight jaw line of the upset young man. "With me working here, we should be able to see each other pretty often, shouldn't we?"

Jimmy's taut face relaxed, and he rested his head against the softness of her hair as he held her close. "Now that I've found you, my Texas beauty, I can't let you go. I couldn't make it without you and your strawberry kisses."

"You don't have to be without me," Grace said. "Ever since you and Brandy rode into my life, I've known I want only you. We'll make this work some way."

"Some way, sweetheart. It has to work." Jimmy found her mouth with his searching lips, and all the passion in their young bodies erupted as the rippling river and singing birds provided accompaniment to their ecstasy.

Grace slowly pulled herself free from their embrace. "I've got to go, Jimbo. My dad's in the restaurant talking to Leota right now. He'll be looking for me, and I have a feeling he had better not see me with you."

Jimmy shook his head and sighed. "I'm sure you're right."

"Don't look so sad. We can see each other often now."

Jimmy's face brightened, and he stepped easily into the saddle and headed down the river trail. Grace watched until he was out of sight. Touching her lips with her fingers as if to seal in the sweetness of his kisses, she turned and ran back toward the lodge. When she emerged from the trees, she slowed to a walk, looking anxiously toward the porch. Just then her father came out of the restaurant looking for her.

"Hey Dad," Grace called, surprised that her voice sounded so normal. She didn't know how it could keep from giving away her emotions.

As she climbed breathlessly up the steps, she was almost afraid to look at her father's face. Fortunately the door opened, and Leota stuck out her head. "See you tomorrow, Grace. Hope to see you soon, too, John."

"You can bet on it," John said with a pleased look on his face as he came down the steps.

Grace quickly followed her father to the car and waved goodbye to Leota. Thank you, dear Mrs. Stevenson, she thought. Dad surely would have noticed something if you hadn't distracted him. Mama used to tell me you don't blab everything you know. I know I am in love with Jimmy Kirkwood, but I don't think I'd better let Dad know it quite yet!

9

The long summer days went by smoothly. Grace learned to drive so she could take her father to work in the morning and then go on to the lodge for her day. A miner who lived in Pecos and worked in Tererro dropped John off at the Holy Ghost turn-off after their shifts were over. Grace's days varied as she sometimes stayed to help in the restaurant after she closed the gift shop.

The Ponderosa Gift Shop was arranged very attractively with brightly woven Indian rugs adorning the walls and expensive turquoise jewelry gleaming inside glass cases. Handmade pottery rested on numerous shelves.

The inventory came from the Santo Domingo, San Felipe, and Tesuque Pueblos. Grace honestly admired their creations, and they seemed to trust her. She dealt mainly with the women in the tribes, and they apparently made the business decisions.

Grace learned the meanings of the designs on merchandise from her Indian suppliers, so she could tell these stories to her prospective buyers. One day as she was assuring a customer that the buffalo on a blanket would keep her in good health in the future, Leota walked in quietly and listened. After the expensive blanket was sold, and the satisfied owner left, Leota said, "Good work! How do you know these stories?"

"Mary Aragon from Santo Domingo tells me most of them," Grace replied. "I enjoy listening to their legends."

"Well, you're doing a good job. The gift shop is starting out very well, and we're building a reputation for quality merchandise. People are driving up from Santa Fe to look over our inventory."

Grace lowered her eyes and smiled self-consciously. "I'm glad you are pleased, Leota. I love the work."

"By the way, how does your dad like his new job?" Leota asked nonchalantly.

"I think he likes it very well. He never really cared for farming. He's happy to be here while my brother runs the farm."

Leota smiled and went clicking off in her high heels. A happy hum reached Grace's ears as her boss went to check on the kitchen help. Some bankers from Santa Fe would be here today for a luncheon, and she wanted things to be extra special for them.

Meanwhile, Grace and Jimmy managed to see each other often. He stopped by the shop regularly, either coming from or going to work, depending on what shift he was working. He often dropped by when he was riding his horse. There were also baseball games nearly every weekend. Grace went to the Sunday games and usually attended the party after the game. Her father had relented a little in his hard stand on Jimmy, but Grace was careful not to let him know how often they saw each other, or how serious their feelings were. As she dusted some expensive Indian vases one day, she smiled and said softly, "I love him so much, my Jimbo."

Grace thought about the coming weekend which she was happily anticipating. The Tererro Miners would be playing in a championship game in Santa Fe. Leota had given her time off to attend an art workshop there on the same day. She knew she and Jimmy would find a way to be together. It would be an exciting time because it was the weekend of the Santa Fe Fiesta.

Just then Grace looked up to see her art teacher, Yvonne Messier, coming through the door. She put her feather duster down and smilingly asked, "And what can I do for you, Madamme?"

Miss Messier carried a picture Grace had recently finished, a black and white ink drawing of a coyote hunched on a mesa howling at the moon. Studying the image, one could almost hear the mournful sound of loneliness echoing over the desert landscape. "I have a suggestion for you," she said. "I would like to frame this picture so you can display it in the hall. I think it will sell."

"Do you really?" Grace gasped. "Do you honestly think someone would buy that picture?"

"It's good," Miss Messier said. "I think it will sell. In fact, I'm going to display some of our other students' works, also. I have talked to Leota, and we can use both sides of the hall for our creations. Isn't that exciting?"

"Oh yes! That's fantastic. But, isn't it going to cost a lot to have the pictures framed?"

"Not that much," Miss Messier said smugly. "I know a framer in Santa Fe who will do it for us very reasonably. He'll exchange art framing for art lessons."

The thought of someone buying her work was more than Grace could fathom. She only knew she felt good all over because life was so wonderful these days. Impulsively, the happy girl ran around the counter and embraced her teacher. "Thank you, Miss Messier!" she said emotionally.

"Careful, Grace. I'm glad you're happy, but I don't want tears on this work of art," she said, holding the picture at arm's length.

"I'm sorry," Grace said as she quickly placed her arms behind her.

"No problema," Miss Messier said with a smile. "I'm glad you like my idea. In another week we'll have some of our class's work on display. And that is exciting for me, also."

As her teacher left, another head appeared in the door. "Time fer my break," Adele said brightly. "Can I come in fer a few minutes?"

"Sure," Grace said with a smile. "I have something I want to talk to you about."

"Go ahead," Adele said as she settled herself on one of the two stools behind the counter.

"I want you to go to Santa Fe with me next Saturday. I'm going to an art workshop there, and when I'm finished we can go to the fiesta for a while. Does that sound exciting?"

Adele's eyes were big as she contemplated this exciting proposal. "I have to work, you know."

"Maybe Leota will give you the time off. That's the day Tererro plays for the baseball championship in Santa Fe. Not too many people will be left in town to come to the lodge. All of Tererro will be at that game. Maybe your mom could cover for you after she finishes her cabin work."

Adele was tempted. But the idea of taking a day off from work to have fun was totally foreign to the girl, and she debated this new concept before saying, "Do you think I really oughta?"

"Of course, you should," Grace replied merrily. "We'll eat Mexican food and dance all night. Doesn't that sound like fun?"

"I'll think on it," Adele said with a serious frown on her face.

"It will be fun," Grace emphasized. "You deserve a change of scene. Come on, be a pal. You can explore Santa Fe while I'm at my workshop. No telling what you will find there. Maybe even a good looking man!"

Adele looked at her friend impatiently. "Grace, you are sech a tease. You know I don't like boys, much less a man. And I cain't dance."

Grace stepped from behind the counter and twirled gracefully around the gift shop. "It's time Adele learned to dance," she sang. "It's time Adele learned to dance and prance; so to Santa Fe we soon will go, and all these things she soon will know."

Grace whirled around the room one more time and then came over to bow before Adele. "May I have this dance, senorita?"

Adele jumped off her stool and headed for the door, her face flaming red. "I've got to git back to work," she said hastily.

"Work hard now, but it's Santa Fe for us this weekend. Don't forget!"

10

As Grace drove down the lane to Adele's house, a little cabin set in the middle of a green meadow with the Pecos River running behind it, Adele was just coming out the door. Grace gave five honks, and Adele covered her ears and scowled. "Get a move on, girl!" Grace called. "It's time to go to Santa Fe!"

Adele was wearing a loose summer dress with her toes poking out the ends of sandals, her red hair falling attractively around her shoulders. "You look very pretty," Grace said as the tall girl slid into the car. She's learning to take care of herself better, Grace thought. She's fixing her hair and pressing her clothes. She's really quite attractive now.

The pink glow of Adele's skin made her appear young and appealing. "Aw, go on," she protested. "I could never be purty."

Grace backed the car up to turn around and spun the wheels as she started back up the driveway. "Shut your mouth, girl. Have you looked in the mirror lately?" Grace said.

Adele's cheeks turned pinker. "I don't look in mirrors very much," she answered.

"Well, try it. You have blossomed, Adele. I tell you no lies."

"Flowers bloom," Adele mumbled. "How could I blossom, fer Pete's sake?"

"Take my word for it," Grace replied, laughing, as she changed the subject. "We're on our way to Santa Fe. Can you believe it?"

"I guess I gotta believe it," Adele replied solemnly.

The girls headed swiftly down the canyon, leaving the high altitude behind. As they drove under steep rocky cliffs, Adele pointed to the road ahead. "Do you know that's the place where Malcolm Dodson was killed?"

"Was he related to Ned Dodson at the store?"

"Yep, he was his brother. One day last summer he was drivin' down this road goin' to Santa Fe to deposit the payroll money in the bank there. Later he was found in his car. He'd been shot. They ain't figured out who done it yet."

"Was his money stolen?" Grace asked, looking at the high cliff to their left with big eyes.

"No, the money was there in the car in a sack. But a bag holdin' the car chains was gone. My daddy says the robber might o' taken the wrong bag."

Grace shivered as she thought of the gory scene. It must have happened before my family came to Tererro, she thought. Poor Mr. Dodson. But she was in too good a mood to let this story dampen her spirits. Her thoughts went soaring ahead to Santa Fe.

"Won't it be fun to spend the night in Santa Fe? It was so nice of Miss Messier to let us stay with her. My dad didn't give his approval at first, but then decided it was okay since he was going with Mr. Cooper up into the wilderness above Cowles for a weekend camping trip. He'll be up there fishing, so we'll have perfect freedom to enjoy the weekend. Isn't that exciting?"

"I guess so," Adele said, doubt in her voice. She had seldom been away from the little cabin by the river and had no idea whether or not she would enjoy an overnight stay. The very thought of it was a little overwhelming to her.

The girls soon crossed the bridge that took them into the little town of Pecos, and Grace pulled up in front of the grocery store. "I didn't have any breakfast," she said. "Let's get us a treat."

As they walked up the steep stone steps into the store, Adele said, "Mama made me eat a bowl o' oatmeal this mornin'. I ain't too hungry."

"I'll bet you would enjoy a strawberry soda pop," Grace said, smiling. "That will be a good way to start our trip."

As they entered the big adobe building, Grace announced to everyone in the store, "We're going to Santa Fe for the fiesta!" But there were only three people to tell this wonderful news to: two older Spanish ladies and the beady eyed cashier. They seemed unimpressed with the big news, so she went to the old barrel filled with ice and soda pop and dug around until she found her favorite. "I think I"ll have a Butterfinger candy bar, too," she said to Adele. "Do you want one?"

Adele looked uncertainly at the soda pop barrel and suddenly thrust her hand in and retrieved an orange drink. "Yes," she said. "And I'll have a Baby Ruth."

The two girls were smiling when they got back into the Studebaker. Grace drove slowly and carefully as she ate her candy and drank her strawberry pop. Adele sat quietly as she savored every bite. Grace knew Adele seldom spent money on things like this. She saved practically every penny of her small checks, and had recently told Grace she had nearly one hundred dollars put away.

Grace had been impressed about her savings, and although her father had always given her money for anything she wanted or needed, she had started setting aside some of her wages, also. She had brought along only a few dollars to spend at the fiesta. Their lodging would cost them nothing, so she needed only a little money. She would enjoy drinks and ice cream and some Mexican food. Her mouth watered at the thought of the spicy food. She had never eaten anything like that in Texas, but she was developing quite a taste for it. Black eyed peas and biscuits are good, she thought, but I'm learning to like pinto beans and tortillas better. Glancing over at Adele she said, "I can't wait to have an enchilada, but with no egg on it."

"I love eggs on enchiladas," Adele replied. "And I like the red chili."

"I'm going to have green chili," Grace said. "Love that green chili. I think it's addicting."

Adele didn't know what that word meant. Grace and her fancy words, she thought.

They soon turned off the main highway to go into Santa Fe on the Old Pecos Trail Road. They passed the capitol building, a pink stucco Spanish style structure. "Someday I'd like to see inside that building," Grace said. "It's such a grand capitol. I'm so glad I'm a New Mexican now!"

Adele wrinkled her brow and looked straight ahead. She had no desire to see inside the government building, and had always been a New Mexican, so she couldn't think of any response to those statements. Sometimes her Texas friend confused her.

The Santa Fe Art School was near the Plaza, and Grace turned right before they got to the square and drove straight to the school. "Here we are!" she announced. "Let's get out and see what's going on. Or you can go on over to the Plaza and walk around there if you'd rather."

"I'll go with you," Adele replied nervously. "Maybe I can do somethin' to help Miss Messier."

As it turned out, Miss Messier needed someone to watch two of the students' young children, so Adele volunteered. The art teacher had wondered what to do with them and was afraid they would be a disaster in the art room. But she hadn't wanted to tell the mothers they couldn't take the class. "You're a godsend," she said to Adele. "Take them over to my house next door. At lunch time you can bring them back here, and they can have some of the sandwiches and donuts I have prepared for the class. Maybe you can take them to the Plaza to play in the afternoon. If they get tired, take them back to my house and put them down for a nap. I really appreciate your doing this for me."

"Glad to do it," Adele said. She was happy to be useful, and she enjoyed little children.

Miss Messier and Grace then went back to the school, as it was time for the workshop to begin. A guest teacher from the university in Albuquerque would conduct the first class.

The early art history of New Mexico would be discussed, as well as the Indian influence on Spanish colonial art. The method of making pottery would be demonstrated, and the students would actually create a pottery piece in the afternoon.

Grace was becoming very interested in the different kinds of pottery the Indians were bringing into the gift shop, and she knew she would enjoy this project. Three of the best pottery makers from the surrounding pueblos would be there to assist the students.

The morning lectures were very informative, and Grace took many notes. As the teacher talked about early Spanish Conquistadores, she found herself interested in history for the first time. When the teacher asked for comments at the end of one of the classes, Grace raised her hand. "New Mexico history is much more interesting than reading about the Pilgrims." When the teacher nodded his head and smiled, she added, "I thought the Pilgrims were the first people to colonize North America, but I know now that the Spanish were here exploring and making settlements before the English settled in Jamestown. And I've also learned that the very first colonists in North America were the Indians. For some reason I had never really understood that."

"I don't think that is stressed in our history textbooks," the teacher said. "And the artwork done here in those early times was more colorful and imaginative than any done in the East." The teacher smiled at Grace. He was a true educator who loved to see the spark of knowledge ignited in his students.

The students were soon busy molding their clay pots and painting designs on them with colors created from plants and soil. The pottery would be left to be fired in the kiln. Grace put handles and a spout on each side of her pot, and one of the assistants told her she had created an Indian wedding vase. "The tradition is that there will be a long and happy marriage if the bride and groom drink simultaneously from each side of the wedding vase on their nuptial night." The story intrigued Grace, and she worked very hard to smooth the clay and paint the designs to perfection.

Around five o'clock the classes were all over, and the students gathered up their notes and thanked the teachers for a rewarding day. "This is the first day of school I have ever enjoyed," Grace told Miss Messier. "I loved the art history lectures, and learning to make pottery was fascinating. I almost wish this day would never end."

"There will be more workshops," Miss Messier assured Grace. "Keep working hard, and in time you can be teaching these classes yourself. You learn fast, and art is obviously your field."

"Me, a teacher!" Grace shook her head. "My father would never believe that."

"I'm serious, Grace," Miss Messier said. "Keep working, and you will have your own studio some day where you can create as well as teach art classes. Or you could teach in an art school like this one."

"No, thank you," Grace declined. "There is only one place I would consider worthy of opening an art studio, and that is near the Pecos. And I know what I would name it: the Pecos Queen. How does that sound?"

"It sounds to me like you've been thinking about this before," Miss Messier said. "Are you going to be in competition with me?"

"Not for a while," Grace said, laughing. "And I really never thought of doing this before. You just inspire me."

"You're the kind of student who inspires me," the teacher replied. "But we'd better check on Adele. Hopefully she still has all her senses. The day went by fast and pleasant for us, but I'm not so sure that's the way it went for her."

Miss Messier and Grace and the two mothers soon found Adele and the children in the back yard happily making dandelion curls. A quick tear came to Grace's eyes at the sight of the green ringlets. The day she and

Adele had sat by the river doing this same thing seemed so long ago. That had been the day her mother died, and her whole life had changed.

After the mothers and children were gone, the girls sat down to relax before supper. "We're going to the cafe on the Plaza and eat Mexican food," Grace explained to Miss Messier.

"Could I come, too?" Miss Messier asked.

"Why surely," Grace spoke slowly.

"Call me Vonnie, please. And, you're probably wondering why I want to go with you."

Grace had wondered, and Vonnie quietly explained, "The truth of the matter is, sometimes teachers' lives are very lonely. We're supposed to be prim and proper, you know, and many people, especially young men, don't find us too alluring."

"But you are very alluring," Grace said. "You look different somehow, and you sound different when you talk."

"I'm French," Vonnie said. "That's why I have the dark hair and eyes and the olive complexion. And that's why I have a little accent. I came to Santa Fe to find the ideal inspirational atmosphere."

Adele had been looking at the art teacher with wide eyes. "Do you like it here?" she blurted out, forgetting her shyness.

"I love it," Vonnie said with a smile. "It's everything I hoped it would be, and more. But the art goes better than the social life. I have no one to go to the fiesta with tonight, and I would appreciate it if you'd let me go with you. I'll treat you to that Mexican supper in appreciation for your taking care of the children today, Adele."

"Oh, come on and go with us," Adele said quickly. "But I have my own money."

"All right, girls. I'll take you up to your room so you can freshen up, and I'll get out of my smock and change clothes. Then we girls will be off to the fiesta!"

When Grace and Adele were alone in their room, they looked at each other and Grace whispered, "Well, we know we are girls, but what about Miss M.? I mean Vonnie. Is she still a girl?"

Adele said serously, "Well, I don't think she is too old. But I never thought o' teachers bein' girls before."

"We may learn a lot of things we didn't know before this adventure is over," Grace said, smiling as she poured water into a deep wash bowl and splashed her face. Then she quickly wiped the cold water off with a towel, and, pink and fresh-faced, she asked the sober Adele, "Aren't you glad we came? Isn't this just too exciting?"

Adele's serious face suddenly broke into a wide grin. "This is the most excitingest thing I've ever done, Grace!"

11

Fiesta time in old Santa Fe! What a gala affair. The two girls from Tererro stood in awe as they watched all the people and took in the sounds and sights. Bands played in the plaza and in the streets while celebrants danced and sang. Smiles and laughter and happy voices filled the air as buyers crowded around the shops offering a variety of food, from Indian bread and Spanish cookies, to plain old American-made ice cream. Brightly colored Mexican blouses and skirts hanging on wires strung along the sidewalks waved gracefully in the balmy New Mexico breeze. Tables on the walkways were loaded with various kinds of pottery from the pueblos, and the space in front of the old Governors' Palace was reserved for Indian women and men to sell their silver and turquoise jewelry. They sat beside their creations, which were displayed on a blanket, and made their sales with few words and fewer smiles. The Spanish music and spicy chili smells in the air combined to make an exciting atmosphere which was infectious to the large crowd of both dark and light skinned revelers.

Later, when Grace, Adele, and Vonnie came out of the Mexican restaurant, they headed for an ice cream stand and waited impatiently in line. "I want a strawberry double dip cone," Grace said to the waitress. "I've been dreaming of this ever since I left Tererro this morning."

The Tererro visitors had gathered in one corner of the Plaza, and the girls drifted over to join them. Vonnie took a lick of her ice cream. "Not as good as French vanilla," she pronounced.

"Lord o' mercy," Adele said as she sampled her chocolate sundae, "I think I've died and gone to heaven. Take a bite o' this, Grace."

Grace opened her mouth wide for the spoonful of ice cream and shut her eyes to more fully enjoy this delicacy. Just as the spoon reached her mouth, she felt a slight nudge behind her, and the ice cream ended up on her nose.

"For heaven's sake!" she exclaimed as she hastily turned around. "What are you doing? You've ruined a good bite of ice cream." She looked up into the amused face of a baseball player.

"But you look good with ice cream on your nose," Jimmy said, laughing. In the next moment he had delicately licked it off, and brown arms of steel encircled her tightly. "And you taste good, too!" he whispered softly in her ear.

Grace stamped her foot. "Jim Kirkwood, I could kill you. You have made me a perfect mess." She pushed back, and her eyes swept over the lithe length of him in his baseball uniform. "You look silly in that get-up with cowboy boots," she said impatiently.

"Can't wear cleats in the Plaza. And I won't take all the credit for making you a mess. But as long as you're a perfect mess, I won't complain." Jimmy grinned down lovingly at Grace and pulled her back into his arms. "Now give me a kiss. You're looking at the winning pitcher. We just beat Las Vegas for the state championship!"

"You won?" Grace asked excitedly. "You're really the state champions?"

"I tell you no lie, girl. Ask all these people here. They came to the game to see me pitch instead of going to a stuffy art class."

Grace made a face at the champion and cleaned her nose on his sleeve before turning her head to the people behind them. They were all watching the pitcher and his girl and were smiling. She gave up trying to clean her face since the harm was already done. Suddenly she put her arms around her tormentor and gave him a solid kiss as the crowd around them laughed and clapped. "Congratulations," she said softly as she looked up into her ball player's dancing brown eyes.

"Thank you, darlin'." Lifting Grace high in his arms, Jimmy held her close and gave her another long kiss while he shielded their faces with his cap. "Folks, meet my girl, Grace Shockey," he finally said. "She's from Texas, and she's my strawberry lovin' doll."

The crowd gave Jimmy and Grace another round of applause, and Jimmy slowly eased his girl away from the crowd.

"Now buy me another ice cream cone since this one is ruined," she said as she dropped her dripping cone in a garbage can and tried to lead him to the ice cream stand.

"I want to dance with you, Tex," Jimmy protested. "Forget about ice cream cones. You're a big girl now, aren't you?"

"I'll forget about it for now," Grace said as he pulled her out in the street to dance.

Jimmy took his partner in his arms just as the band started playing the old Spanish song, "Cielito Lindo." He held her close, and the smell of her clean dark hair with a hint of strawberry flavor made him forget his hard fought battle for the baseball championship. "You feel so good, darlin'," he whispered. "I don't want this dance to ever be over."

The young couple danced through two more pieces, and then the ball player suddenly realized how tired he was. "I'll buy you some ice cream, and we can sit down and rest a while. It's been a long day, Tex. I hope you don't mind."

"I don't care what I do as long as I'm with you," Grace said softly.

"You are an angel, afterall, instead of the rebel I thought you were."

"And you are incorrigible."

"I'm not sure what that means, but I deny that accusation."

Grace suddenly thought about her friends and looked through the crowd trying to find them. Finally she spotted Adele's red head looming above the other dancers. "She's dancing with Eric Anderson," she said in surprise. She had seen Eric around the lodge lately. "Aha!" she announced with sudden insight. "Eric has been coming to see Adele, and she hasn't told me a word."

"What are you talking about? Jimmy asked.

"Never mind," Grace said. "I just figured something out. Where is Vonnie?"

"You mean the art teacher, Miss Messier?"

"Yes, her first name is Yvonne, but we call her Vonnie. She came with us tonight."

Just then Vonnie appeared with a husky partner by her side. She turned a vivacious smile their way. "Grace, this is Shoney Terrell."

"I've seen him at the lodge," Grace said. "Jimmy, do you know him?"

"Of course," Jimmy said. "He's my shift boss."

"Good game," Shoney said as he extended his hand to Jimmy. "I'll have to take it a little easy on you at work on Monday." The shift boss smiled, and Grace noticed how impressive he was. Dark hair, blue eyes that looked straight through you, broad shoulders, thick chest, no hips. Just right for Vonnie, Grace thought.

"Excuse us for a minute," Shoney said as he led Jimmy away. Grace was impressed with the smooth powerful movements of the big man as they left. Just like a lynx, she thought.

Turning to Vonnie, Grace remarked, "You captured one of our prizes tonight. Everyone respects Shoney, and nobody gives him any guff. The talk is that he learned to box in the Army and did some professional fighting after he got out of the Service."

"Really?" Vonnie said. "I just noticed his beautiful blue eyes."

"I'll bet you did," Grace replied, smiling.

Vonnie and Grace kept their eyes on Adele while the men talked. "Eric is one of three Swedish brothers who work at the mine," Grace explained. "They're known as hard workers who never spend a penny needlessly. Let's see if Eric spends any money on Adele."

Grace and Vonnie watched Eric and Adele trying to dance a schottische. Adele attempted to follow her partner's long legs, but her awkward feet got in the way. "I'm afraid she's going to trip him, and they'll both fall," Grace giggled.

Realizing this dance could end in disaster, Eric suddenly stopped and said, "Is 'ust too fast. We rest now." Eric and Adele headed for Grace and Vonnie's table.

Grace couldn't resist a comment. "You looked good out there."

Adele turned red and her icy blue eyes shot daggers at her friend. Grace knew she'd better say nothing else.

Grace's eyes drifted over to where Jimmy and Shoney were standing. Just then, they turned and walked over to a man leaning against a tree in the Plaza. Grace couldn't hear the words, but she instinctively knew this was not a friendly conversation. At that moment another man joined them, and he began exchanging heated remarks with the two miners. Shoney edged forward and stood poised for action as the two men glared at him, but they finally turned and walked off. Shoney and Jimmy talked together for a short time and then ambled back to the table.

"Sorry about that," Shoney apologized. "We needed to get a clear message to those two yahoos."

"What about?" Vonnie asked.

"First I told the one fellow to stay away from you. I saw him trying to get you to dance with him earlier. Then I told both of them to stay away from the mine. We don't need any trouble makers around there," Shoney said with a set jaw and hard blue eyes.

"Oh," Vonnie said quietly. Grace said nothing, but she knew this encounter was serious. Adele and Eric looked uncomfortable.

Jimmy broke the awkward silence with an attempt to recapture the festive mood. "It will soon be time for Zozobra to be burned. Let's walk to the other end of the park where we can get a better view."

"Who is Zozobra?" Grace asked.

"Oh, he's Old Man Gloom," Jimmy explained. "It's a tradition each year to build a large grumpy looking creature out of wire and paper mache. At the height of the fiesta celebration the creature is set afire and burned. The idea is that all our troubles go up with the fire and smoke of Zozobra. Do you have any worries you want to get rid of tonight?"

"I suppose," Grace said quietly. "But its a pretty perfect night, really."

"For me, too," Jimmy said as he put his arm around the radiant girl. "But it won't hurt to let the old man take away whatever troubles we have. What do you think, folks?"

"Sounds good to me," Vonnie said.

"Sounds dumb to me," Adele said grumpily.

"'Tis 'ust for fun," Eric rebuked Adele.

"And fun it will be," Shoney said in his deep voice. "There goes Zozobra!"

The group stood transfixed as the giant figure suddenly burst into flames that shot high into the sky. The tongues of fire illuminated the faces of the crowd, and everyone started shouting and shaking their fists in upward motions. "Go, Zozobra! Go, Zozobra! Go away, Mr. Gloom!"

The smoke and flames climbed high in the sky as the giant figure turned into ashes. Then as suddenly as the fire had escalated, it began to burn down to the elated shouts of the crowd.

"Zozobra is gone. Everyone must have a happy face now," Vonnie said. "It's getting late, boys, and I must take my girls home. Do you want to walk with us, gentlemen?"

"It would be our pleasure," Shoney said. "I think we'd better get these girls and boys home, Vonnie. Maybe you and I are old enough to stay up a little longer."

"Oh, sure," Jimmy laughed. "I think we should stay up and chaperone you two."

"Don't make me pull rank on you, young man," Shoney said, shaking his finger at Jimmy.

The couples walked slowly down San Francisco Street to Vonnie's house, but Jimmy and Grace lingered behind and stopped under a huge elm tree. The moon was now shining down to light the blackness after Zozobra's spectacular performance. As the soft rays shone on Grace's upturned face, Jimmy said softly, "This is the most perfect day of my life. I helped win the baseball championship for my team, and I have the prettiest girl in the Pecos Valley by my side. It just don't get no better than this, Tex."

"I love you, Jimbo," Grace whispered after a long kiss, as she snuggled securely in his strong arms.

"Grace, we've got to get married. I can't stand it any longer. I want you with me."

Grace listened to his words and drowned in his passionate kisses. At last she answered breathlessly, "Of course, we'll get married. I've known that from the first day I saw you. It's always been written in the stars that we would be married. Oh yes, Jimmy Kirkwood, I most certainly will marry you!"

12

The fiesta girls were back home by noon the next day, having driven up the canyon in thoughtful silence as each pondered the events of the night before. Grace glanced over at Adele. She's thinking about Eric, she thought. I'll bet she didn't know he existed until last night, even though he's been hanging around the lodge.

As for her own feelings, Grace realized she had never before experienced the emotions that were now sweeping over her. She felt overwhelmed with anticipation, wild abandon, and glorious awe, all at the same time. I'm going to be Jimmy's wife! she told herself over and over. I know this is right. I've never felt so right in my whole life. I was born to be Jimmy Kirkwood's wife.

But a nagging thought kept invading her jubilation. What about Dad? She knew he was not going to approve. But I'm nineteen, she rebelliously told herself, and I can do as I please.

"Thanks," Adele said when Grace dropped her off at home. "It was fun. See you at work on Monday." She walked briskly toward her house, eager to get back to her world of reality.

John Shockey was nowhere to be seen when Grace arrived at their mountain cabin. Dad's probably getting in all the fishing he can today, she thought. I think I'll change clothes and saddle up Duchess and take a ride. There can't possibly be too many of these perfect fall days left.

Duchess was eager for an outing, and the excited mare pawed the ground nervously as Grace saddled and bridled her. Grace then tightened the cinch and stepped up into the saddle. She leaned over for a moment, gently patting the mare's neck. "Good girl," she said softly. "Easy, girl. Easy, Dutch."

Suddenly the familiar voice of Jimmy Kirkwood called to her from the road. "Hello, Tex. I'm taking a victory ride today. Want to join me?"

Grace quickly turned Duchess and hurried to greet Jimmy. "We had the same idea, Duchess and me," she said smiling. "See how our minds work together!"

"I'll open the gate for you, Babe," Jimmy said as he pulled the post away from the wire holder. He then closed the gate, remounted, and brushed Grace's cheek with a kiss just before the two horses fell into a brisk walk down the road.

"Where are we going?" Grace asked above the whinny of her mare.

"Down to the river," Jimmy replied. "Brandy and I need some air today after the bright lights of the city. It's good to come home and relax."

"I know," Grace agreed. "I'd never want to live in a big town all the time. Tererro suits me."

"Indian Creek suits me fine. I'll have to take you there one of these days soon."

Grace smiled and pictured his home. Soon my home, too! The thought made her shiver with anticipation.

The riders settled into a comfortable silence until they reached the Pecos Road and crossed down to the river. "I have an idea. Let's ride up to Indian Cave," Grace shouted above the noise of the river. "Do you have a flashlight?"

"Sure thing. But you'll have to show me the way," Jimmy shouted back.

"It's past the dairy and up Willow Creek a little ways," Grace said, taking the lead.

As they passed the Owens' house, Grace wondered how Monte May was doing. She hadn't thought about her old friend since she had gone to work. I suppose she's in Albuquerque in school now, she mused. And her brothers would be back in high school.

The horses climbed the steep incline to the cave. Grace stopped Duchess and pointed to the opening. "Here we are. Let's go exploring."

They tied up their horses and walked over to the gaping hole in the mountain. "None of your nonsense, do you understand?" Grace said firmly as she turned to Jimmy. "It's pitch dark in there, and I want you to promise the flashlight will be on at all times."

"Sure," Jimmy agreed, smiling, but as they entered the cave he went back on his word. "I can't help it if the batteries don't work," he said, laughing.

Grace wheeled around to turn back, but Jimmy quickly snapped the light back on. "Sorry. I won't do that anymore. I was just teasing."

Grace directed a swift kick at his backside, and Jimmy almost caught her foot. "Relax, Babe," he said.

As the two laughing explorers moved deeper into the engulfing blackness, Grace told Jimmy about the time her father had brought Monte May and her there earlier in the summer. "We left a candle. I hope it's still here."

"We'll just see about that," Jimmy responded.

When they came to the point where the cave branched into two passageways, Grace asked Jimmy to shine the flashlight on the wall. "Sure enough!" she said. "There's the candle we left. And there should be some matches too."

Jimmy reached up and carefully felt around the base of the candle. "Here they are," he said. "Hold the flashlight while I light it."

Candlelight soon bathed the young couple in a soft lover's glow. "It seems like forever since I held you like this," Jimmy said as he pulled Grace close. Their lips met, and the same charged magic was there, even in a dark gloomy cave.

Jimmy slowly pulled back and looked down at Grace. "I told myself this morning I must have dreamed what happened last night. You did say you love me and will marry me, didn't you?"

"I did, if you truly love me and want me for your wife."

"I do, Grace. I do." Yearning lips again found each other.

"You're going to have to talk to my dad, you know," Grace said, gently pulling away.

"I know, and I will. But, I've got to build a room on my cabin if a wife will be living there. We may not be able to get married for a while."

"How long will it take you to build that room?"

"Maybe three months. Now that baseball season is over, I will have some time to work on it."

"That's all right," Grace said with a sigh. "I'd move in that cabin today, whether it has another room or not."

Jimmy held her face in his hands. "But I don't have a bedroom now. I sleep in the living room. We need a special private bedroom. That's what I'll be building."

Grace felt hot color in her face. "Don't tell Dad we can't get married until you build us a bedroom."

"Well, it's the truth," Jimmy said. "What's wrong with that?"

I'm afraid Dad would find it hard to imagine his daughter marrying a man who has no bedroom for her, she thought as she hugged him tightly.

Jimmy moved the flashlight beam around the cave as he held Grace with one arm. Suddenly the light fell on a dark object on the floor of the cave a few feet down the passageway to the right. "There's something there," he said. "Stay here by the candle, and I'll see what it is."

Grace followed Jimmy's outline as he studied the dark mass. "That's strange," he said, almost talking to himself as he returned. "What would a sack of car chains be doing in here?"

Then Grace remembered the story about the murder of the storekeeper. "Adele told me her father thinks the murderer of Malcolm Dodson picked up a sack of car chains by mistake instead of the bag of money. Did you ever hear that?"

"No," Jimmy said, "but it makes sense." He then looked over at the car chains for a moment. "Let's get out of here, Babe." He reached for the candle and blew it out, quickly returning it to the ledge.

Grace swiftly followed behind Jimmy as he led the way. Again, as on her first trip into the cave, the circle of light at the end of the passageway was a welcome sight, indicating the entrance was near.

They came out into the bright light and blinked with relief. "I don't care much for caves," Jimmy said breathlessly. "Let's get back to your house. Maybe your dad is there by now."

"I don't know who's scarier, my dad or the cave," Grace said with a shudder as she stepped up into her saddle.

"Yeah," Jimmy said between his teeth as he turned his horse. "We'll have to hurry because I've got to make a call to the deputy sheriff in Pecos."

Grace didn't ask, but she knew the call would be about the car chains.

No more conversation was exchanged until the riders were back on the road. "Don't tell anyone about what we saw," Jimmy said seriously. "And don't be going in that cave by yourself."

"I won't," Grace said softly. "I hope you're not upset at me for taking you there. I just thought it would be an interesting place to show you."

"Very interesting," Jimmy agreed with a frown on his face.

When they turned off the road at the Holy Ghost sign, Jimmy glanced up at the white building on the hill to the right. "I could make a call from there," he said, "but maybe I'd better go on to the lodge. I wouldn't want to tie up the telephone line at the hospital."

As they rode on up the road, Grace could see the Studebaker parked in front of their cabin. "Dad's home," she said in a worried voice.

"Good," Jimmy said. "We can talk to him right now."

Jimmy tied his horse to the fence, got off and opened the gate for Grace. Then he helped her take the saddle and bridle off Duchess. "I'll carry in your tack for you. Where do you keep it?"

"In the shed," Grace said.

But just then, John Shockey came out of the cabin and walked toward them. He was brown and unshaven from his days in the wilderness. His eyes were direct and questioning. "Where have you been? I thought you would be here when I got home," were his impatient words.

"I got back a little after noon," Grace said evenly.

"We decided to go for a ride up to Indian Cave," Jimmy broke in with a steady voice. "Sir, we need to talk to you."

John's eyes took on a wary expression. "I'm listening," he said.

"Well, first of all," Jimmy said with a twinkle in his eyes, "We won the championship in Santa Fe Saturday. The Tererro Miners are now state baseball champions."

"Congratulations," John said in a flat voice. "What else do you have to say?"

Jimmy took a step forward, looking the older man straight in the eyes. "Grace and I are in love, Mr. Shockey, and we have decided we want to get married."

John let out a sigh before his head dropped on his chest. Slowly he looked up, his eyes directed at Jimmy with shock and anger. "My daughter is too young to marry anyone," he said tightly.

"I know she's young, sir," Jimmy said slowly. "Hell, I'm pretty young myself." Instantly he knew he should not have said it that way. "But," he continued, "we are in love, and we want to get married." He paused and looked at John steadily. "And we want your blessing," he added earnestly.

John Shockey looked sadly off into space. Grace's heart broke for her father. "We aren't going to do it for a while, Dad," she said quickly. "Jimmy has some work he has to do on his house."

John's eyes finally returned to his daughter. "I suppose it's a company house," he said coldly.

"No sir," Jimmy replied in a clear voice. "I own a few acres up Indian Creek. I have a cabin on my land, but I'll have to build another room if I'm going to have a wife."

John winced. "We should have gone back to Texas," he said in a harsh voice. "We should never have stayed here. What would your mother think, Grace?"

"She would be happy for me," Grace replied, her voice shaking. "She was eighteen when she married you, Dad, and I'm sure she never regretted it."

Grace's mother had told her the story of meeting her father at a dance in Houston. John had seen her across the room, a tall girl with cascades of red-gold curls down her back, and he had told a friend, "That's the girl I will marry." He married her a short time later, in spite of her father's protests.

John shook his head and struggled to get control of his thoughts and words. "All right, Jimmy. Thank you for telling me. I just ask you to wait a year to make sure this is what you both want. I don't think that's an unreasonable request."

"It certainly isn't, sir," Jimmy replied, taking a deep breath.

"Do I have your hand on it?" John asked in a steely voice.

Jimmy stuck out his right hand. "You have my hand and my word on it, Mr. Shockey."

The two men shook hands, the older man with shoulders slightly sagging, and the younger one standing straight and proud. Their eyes locked for an instant, and then John Shockey withdrew his hand, turned, and walked slowly to the house. Grace followed him, waving a silent goodbye to Jimmy.

When they got inside, John went to the waterstand, filled the washpan with cold water, and noisily doused his face and head. He scrubbed his wet face and hair with a towel and ran a comb through his hair, parting it in the usual way. Only then did he turn to Grace. He faced her with tears in his eyes, and silently held out his arms. As she rushed into his embrace he said brokenly, "It's not easy for a man to give up his only daughter, especially when he just gave up her mother."

"I know, Dad," Grace said as she stroked his shaking shoulders. "I know, Dad."

13

Sunday was a good time for sleeping, Grace had always thought. And now that she was working, it was the one day she could relax.

I'm thankful I'm in New Mexico, she thought. If I still lived in Texas, I'd have to get up and go to church. Her parents were long-time loyal Baptist members. There was no Baptist Church closer than Santa Fe, so they had stopped making the trip after her mother's health deteriorated. There was a Community Sunday School in the high school auditorium which she had attended before her mother died, but her father seemed to have forgotten about it. Grace didn't remind him because she disliked Sunday School almost as much as she disliked regular school.

On this morning she lay in bed studying the knotty pine ceiling and deciding what she would do. She knew she would ride; she rode every Sunday. The question was, where?

She decided to go up to the Owens' house to see if Monte May had come home for the weekend. Even if she hadn't, it was always good to see the rest of the family. Mr. and Mrs. Owens were both very sweet to her, and the boys were in seventh heaven when she was around. She enjoyed their admiration and was actually quite fond of them. They seemed like younger brothers to her and always gave her the news from her old high school. Miss Phipps was still piloting the school with an iron hand. She's omnipotent, Grace thought with a shudder. She'll be there forever. Poor kids!

Grace quickly shook off the thoughts about Miss Phipps as she jumped out of bed and pulled some riding britches and a warm shirt out of her dresser drawer. She dressed quickly in her cold bedroom, pulling on wool socks and riding boots. Then she headed for the kitchen washstand to splash away the lethargy and sleepiness.

"Mornin', Dad," she called as she poured hot water from the tea kettle into the washbasin and then added a couple of dippers of cold water so the temperature would be just right to wash her face.

"Mornin,' sunshine," was her father's cheery reply. "There's bacon, eggs, and toast in the warming oven." John was sitting on the living room couch reading and listening to the "Old Time Gospel Hour" on the radio.

Moments later, Grace dried her face and hands and ran a brush over her silky dark hair. She stroked it straight back and then pulled a few locks to the left side, partially down over her eye. She lowered her head and looked into the mirror with a flirty expression. She liked what she saw and threw her hair back, giving herself a big smile.

As she placed her breakfast on the table, she called to her father, "Thanks so much, Dad. This looks scrumptious."

Grace finished her meal of bacon and eggs with toast and raspberry jelly. Mom made this jelly for us, she thought. Her hands put all these ingredients together, and they taste so good. Then an interesting thought came into her mind. Mama's going to be with me all day because I have her jelly in my tummy. That was a comforting idea, and Grace smiled because she felt her day was starting right.

As Grace quickly washed her dishes in the warm dishpan of water her dad had left on the stove, she called out, "I'm going riding, Dad. I'll head up to the dairy and see if the Owenses are home. I'll probably be gone most of the day."

"All right," John Shockey acknowledged from the other room.

Not one question? Grace thought as she went toward the shed to get her saddle and bridle. He's certainly acting more mellow these days.

Indian summer in Holy Ghost Canyon was spectacular. The evergreens were always the same, but the berry bushes and quaking aspen trees and scrub oaks were going through dramatic color transformations from dark red to golden yellow. The vibrant hues they painted among the fir greens made the forest come alive with dramatic mystery. Their last costume party before they are stifled for the winter, Grace told herself. I must paint this picture for my next art class.

Duchess seemed eager to get out of her pasture and enjoy a fall ride, so the twosome started down the road with light steps. The words from a song she had heard on the radio recently on the Carter Family Show from Del Rio, Texas, came to her mind:

"Beautiful, beautiful brown eyes,
Beautiful, beautiful brown eyes,
Beautiful, beautiful brown eyes,
I'll never love blue eyes again."

After singing the other verses to the song and repeating the chorus, she smiled and said aloud, "That's for you, Jimmy Kirkwood. That's for you and those beautiful brown eyes of yours."

It was only a few more minutes until Grace was at the front porch of the Owens' home. There was no sign of life except the lazy collie dog resting in the shade on the porch, barking a half-hearted warning to her. "Hello yourself, Sandy," Grace said, greeting the family watchdog. "Where's Monte May?"

Sandy slowly wagged her bushy tail, and Grace could see that no one was home. Maybe they're visiting Monte May in Albuquerque, she thought. Or they went to Santa Fe to church.

"Oh well," she said aloud as she turned Duchess. "There must be somebody else I can visit. 'Bye, Sandy."

Duchess plodded back to the Pecos Road as Grace tossed some ideas around in her head. I know Jimmy is still asleep. He's on midnight shift now so I can't visit him, she thought.

As Duchess crossed the bridge spanning the Pecos River, Grace suddenly knew what she would do. I'll ride down to see Adele, she thought. We need to have a visit anyway. She's been so busy at work I never get to talk to her. Anyway she seems pretty preoccupied and tight-lipped these days. I'll spend the afternoon with her and then ride by Jimmy's cabin on my way home. Grace no longer worried about what her father thought of Jimmy. He hadn't even mentioned him lately. But then they weren't conversing very much these days. He was working long hours on his job, and Grace was often asleep by the time he got home.

Grace rode two miles down the road to the Ponderosa Lodge and passed it without a second look. It was good not to have to be there today. She smiled as she glanced at Jimmy's cabin and visualized him sleeping after his long shift. See you later, Jimbo, she promised herself.

Riding the remaining three miles to Adele's house, Grace's attention turned to the mountain colors and smells. "Fall on the Pecos is gorgeous," she told the world in general, and then said to the little animal that darted across the road in front of them and skipped up a tree, "Run fast, little chipmunk. You'd better get your nest filled with nuts and berries for the winter."

A small Catholic Church appeared on the right, built from the same sandstone it stood upon. Grace knew this was an old church, but a few people still attended it each Sunday. A guilty feeling settled over her as she quickly rode past. It had been a long time since she had been in a church; actually, not since her mother's funeral. She knew her father would never go to a Catholic Church, but she would like to visit it someday. It looked peaceful and solid, and it seemed in a perfect setting for a house of God, overlooking the meadow with the rugged mountains rising steeply behind the river. I think God is in that church and watching over all of us who live on the Pecos, Grace assured herself.

When she turned her horse down the lane leading across the green meadow to Adele's home, Grace felt her spirits rising as she thought of visiting with her good friend. She raised a cupped hand to her mouth and shouted, "Hello!"

Adele instantly appeared in the doorway of the log cabin and raised her hand in greeting. Grace dismounted near a scrub oak tree and tied Duchess to one of the branches.

"Lord o' mercy, what are you doin' here?" Adele asked.

"I've come to visit you, silly. Isn't that all right?"

"Well, I guess so," Adele said. "But I'm makin' bread and cleanin' the house. Mama and Poppy are both workin'."

"I'll help you," Grace said, smiling. "You can teach me how to make bread."

Adele's plain face brightened. "Shore, I'll learn ya'. It's easy."

"Well, I need to know how so I can bake it for Jimmy," Grace said casually as she followed Adele into the cabin. The large room they entered served as both a living room and a kitchen.

"Well, ya' should, by rights, be bakin' it fer yore daddy now," Adele said solemnly.

"Well, I need to learn how first," Grace said. "My mama didn't teach me, and besides, she made mostly cornbread and biscuits."

"Yore pore daddy," Adele said, sniffing. "Them kinds o' bread will choke you within a' inch o' yore life."

Grace gave Adele a long-suffering look. "No Adele, my daddy never did get choked, and neither did I. And now we have to buy store-bought bread, so there's no danger of us choking. Just quit worrying about us and tell me what you've got in those bowls," Grace said, pointing to two large mixing bowls on the homemade wooden table.

Adele quickly went around the table, picking up a large metal spoon and stirring the contents in one container. "In this here bowl, I have flour, five cups. In this here other bowl," she continued, pointing, "I have one and a half cups o' warm water, not too hot, mind you, one tablespoon o' sugar, one teaspoon o' salt, one tablespoon o' melted lard, and one cake o' yeast."

"That sounds easy," Grace said. "Flour, water, yeast, sugar, lard, and salt."

Adele looked at Grace and frowned. "Shore, they ain't many ingredients, but you have to do the mixin' right. Now watch me."

Grace did as she was told as Adele poured flour into the liquid mixture. She added a cup at a time and stirred the contents briskly with a big spoon each time more was added.

When the dough became too thick to stir, Adele sprinkled flour on the table and poured the dough out.

"You have to work the bread now," Adele explained as she pushed the dough backwards and forwards, working more flour into the thin mixture. "You have to do this until the dough is thick and smooth and not sticky anymore. Good bread takes a lot o' workin'." She stepped back and instructed Grace, "You do it a while."

Grace started pushing the dough around. "Use yore muscles," Adele directed. "You've got more stren'th in yore hands than that."

Grace quickly bore down, pushing the dough vigorously backward and forward. Adele's instructions had irritated her, and she was determined to show that she wasn't helpless. Her wrists grew tired immediately, but she kept kneading and was glad when Adele asked, "Does the dough feel smooth now?"

Grace heaved a sigh of relief and stepped back. "See for yourself."

Adele gave the dough a few more turns. "Wipe the flour out o' that other bowl and spread some lard over the bottom and sides of it. We'll put this here dough in there to raise."

Soon Grace set the prepared bowl in front of Adele, who plumped the round ball of dough into the container. "We'll cover the dough with a cuptowel and set it in this patch o' sunlight comin' in the winder," Adele said in a satisfied voice. "We'll let it raise fer 'bout a hour," she continued, 'til it's 'bout twice as big as it is now. Then we'll work it agin."

"That's all there is to it?" Grace asked as she wiped lard from her hands.

"That's it," Adele said with a smile. "Now I gotta straighten up this house. Do you want to sweep the floor while I make the beds and pick up things?"

"Sure," Grace said with much enthusiasm as she took the broom and started sweeping toward the back door. After she had swept the dirt out the door, she saw the floor was still streaked with small particles she had missed, so she took a dishrag and wiped up flour spills around the table. After a few more swipes with the broom, the floor looked better. "I'm finished," she yelled toward the bedroom.

"Look outside the back door, and you'll see a pan and a mop hangin' on the wall," Adele yelled back. "Bring 'em in an' fill the pan with warm water from the tea kettle. Put some soap in yore water an' mop the kitchen."

"Lordy," Grace grumbled. "I came down here to visit, not to work."

"Wha'ja say?" Adele yelled back.

"Nothing," Grace said petulantly.

Adele soon came out of the bedroom. "Good job," she said, looking around at the clean kitchen. "You might make a wife fer Jimmy Kirkwood after all."

"I can make a very good wife for him," Grace said with certainty. "But probably not as good a wife at cleaning as you will be for Eric," she added slyly.

Adele's face turned beet red, and she moved her back to Grace as she threw a load of soiled clothes into a basket inside a storage closet. She paused for a moment. "I should wash this afternoon, but I'll do it after supper. Let's go fishin'." She stared at Grace. "I suppose I'll have to teach you how to fish, too."

"I suppose you will," Grace giggled. "Maybe you'll tell me a little more about Eric when we go down to the river," she added as she followed Adele outside.

Adele ignored this comment and took two fishing poles down from the wall. "Grab that shovel layin' there. We've gotta dig some worms," she said, picking up a tomato can lying by a fish basket.

In a low grassy spot near the river, Adele turned up the moist black earth with her shovel and told Grace to pick out the exposed fat worms that tried to pull themselves back into the dirt. They had a can full of wrigglers in no time, and Adele baited their hooks while Grace stood quietly shuddering.

"You do beat all," Adele said as she handed the reluctant fisherman's baited hook to her. "Do you think that worm is goin' to bite you?"

Grace frowned at her tormentor and threw her line in the water. "No!" Adele said impatiently. "Watch me. You never would catch a fish that way if you fished til Doom's Day."

Adele then held her pole with one hand and pulled the line out with the other. She quickly pulled part of the line back, holding it away from the pole, and lifting it back. She instantly thrust the pole forward, turning loose of the line at the same time. The line swished out over the water, and the hook dropped silently down into the ripples. Adele walked along the bank following her hook as it bobbed down the river. She then let it swirl around a rock, and as it drifted to the front of the rock, the line suddenly tightened, and Adele pulled the pole back sharply. "He took the bait! I got 'im!"

Grace was fascinated as Adele pulled in the fish slowly and quickly flipped it out on the bank. "Grab 'im!" she yelled as the fish flopped back toward the river. In a moment, Grace had thrown her pole down and had dived for the fish, but it slithered through her hands.

Adele was prepared. She dropped her pole, grabbed the line, and pulled the fish back. She immediately clenched both hands around her struggling catch, and thrusting a thumb into his gill, she pulled his head back and quickly broke his neck. Tugging the hook out of his throat she said as she held him up, "He's a beauty—a native trout. He'll taste good for supper." She broke off a stick from a small shrub by the water and ran it through the fish's mouth and head.

"We'll leave him here in this shaller water," she told Grace. "He won't dry up that way."

Grace looked over at the prize Adele had caught so fast and made up her mind. "I want to catch the next one," she said. "Show me where to put my line in."

Adele walked down the river a short distance. "There's a hole here. Why don't you jest sit down and put yore line in and let it float around on the bottom. A fish may come up and take it if'n you're very still."

Grace did as she was told, and Adele moved further down the river, stopping to cast out into the center ripples. Grace sat quietly and expectantly, holding fast to her pole. The shimmering water reminded her of a sea of diamonds. The soft musical sounds the river made as it meandered through the meadow suggested an angel's choir. Heaven must look a lot like this, Grace thought. Mama will be fishing every day.

Her thoughts were suddenly interrupted by a strong pull on her line. She jumped up and yelled, "Adele, I've got a fish. Come and help me!"

"Jest pull 'im out," came the answer.

"I don't know how," Grace called frantically, reeling in her line as best she could. She saw the fish as she pulled him closer. The trout she had hooked was long and silver and twisting and turning. A sudden determination swept over Grace, and she gave the line a sharp tug, and the fish flopped onto the grass. She quickly dropped her pole and knelt down by her watery treasure. "Don't you even try," she ordered as she struggled to hold on to the slippery fish. "You're mine!"

Adele came running and took over the fish struggle, swiftly breaking the fish's neck, removing the hook, and holding him up for inspection. "He's bigger'n mine," she said. "You done good, girl!"

Grace then placed her prize on the stick with Adele's fish. "I need another worm on my hook," Grace said as Adele started back down the river.

"Bring your pole down here," Adele replied.

Adele baited her hook, and Grace returned to her spot and put the line back in. She sat down on a rock and leaned against a tree. "I'll take that fish to Jimmy for his supper," she thought as she relaxed, enjoying the satisfaction of her catch.

A short time later Grace was suddenly brought back to reality as Adele yelled, "I'm going back to the house to work my bread dough again. You keep fishin'." Looking back over her shoulder she added, "Were you asleep?"

Grace shook her head.

"No? Jest dreamin' o' Jimmy, right?"

Grace reached down and threw a handful of sand and pebbles in Adele's direction. "Get out of here," she replied, laughing. "Go tend to your bread."

When Adele returned, the girls fished another hour and Adele caught two more. Grace's luck had run out. "That's all right for the first time," Adele assured her friend. "You'll do better next time."

Adele then took a sharp knife out of her pocket and squatted beside the river to clean the fish. She made a cut on the underbody near the tail, and with a deft movement cut a slash from one end of the fish to his head. She pulled the entrails out swiftly and then washed the fish in the river. It took her about two minutes to finish the job.

"You're a fast worker," Grace commented with admiration.

"It's easy as pie," Adele said. "You can do it."

Grace shook her head. "I think I'll leave that to Jimmy."

When they got back to the cabin, Adele took the fish to the cooler by the back door. It was a rectangular structure rising about three feet off the ground. Sawdust had been packed between the double walls. A couple of blocks of ice bought from the iceman and set inside kept the contents cold.

Adele washed her hands with Lava soap and then started to work on the bread. She formed some of the dough into a pan of rolls and put what was left into loaf pans. "We'll have fresh rolls fer supper and two loaves o' bread fer another day." she said. "Well, jest one more loaf, really, cuz I'm goin' to give you one of 'em."

The girls then played dominoes while they waited for the dough to rise enough to be cooked. "You may be a better fisherman than me," Grace said, "but I can beat you in dominoes."

By the time the bread had doubled its size a second time, the girls had played three games, Grace winning them all. "I told you," she reminded her friend. "I almost skunked you in that last game. You barely got a hundred points."

"Hmf!" Adele said as she got up to put the bread in the oven.

"Sit down and tell me about Eric," Grace said as she put the dominos back in their box. "Are you still seeing him?"

Adele sat down and faced her friend with an exasperated look on her face. "Yes, I see him once in a while, and we write letters, if you must know."

"Do you like him?" Grace asked, smiling.

"Did you ever stop to think this might not be any o' yore bizness?" Adele said.

"Adele, I'm your friend," Grace said. "You can tell me. I'll tell you about Jimmy and me."

"There ain't nothin' to tell," Adele persisted. "Now, tell me 'bout yore romance."

"I'll tell you very plainly, Adele, that I am in love," Grace said, the words rushing out of her mouth. "Jimmy has asked me to marry him, and I have said I will do just that. But we have to wait a while until he gets another room built on his house."

Adele looked surprised at this news from her friend. "Well, you'd better learn to bake bread, all right," she finally said, with big eyes.

"I know," Grace agreed, laughing. "You're going to have to come up to Indian Creek and help me with more than just baking bread."

"I'm sure I will," Adele replied seriously. "I think you are goin' to need a whale o' help."

"I'm a fast learner," Grace insisted, not liking the sound of doubt in her friend's voice.

Adele shook her head as she got up to take the bread out of the oven. She then smeared the tops of the rolls and loaves with butter and turned the sweet smelling finished products out on the table.

"I'll have to admit that yeast bread smells better than biscuits or cornbread," Grace observed.

"This here loaf is fer you," Adele said as she wrapped it in wax paper.

"Wonderful!" Grace said. "You can keep my fish and I'll take this bread to Jimmy for a treat."

"I'll give you some currant jam to eat with it," Adele said. "That will give you both a mighty nice treat."

🍎 🍎 🍎

As Grace tied Duchess to a pole in front of Jimmy's cabin, she could hardly wait to see her sweetheart. She knocked twice before she finally heard a sleepy voice from inside. "Who is it?"

"It's Grace," she said. "I have a surprise for you."

"Just a minute," came the groggy reply.

Grace waited impatiently for what seemed like an hour to her before the door opened slowly, and a tousled-headed Jimmy stood there welcoming her with a tired grin. "I can't believe you're here, Tex. What have you got there?"

"Invite me in, and I'll show you," Grace said as he stepped back from the door.

"Don't mind the messy cabin," Jimmy said as he pushed the curtains back from a single window. "I worked last night."

"I know," Grace said. "But I thought you would be up by now." She kept her head turned to avoid looking at the disheveled blankets on his bed.

"Well, I should have been getting up about now," Jimmy said.

"I'm sorry I woke you."

"It's all right," he said with a smile. "I'll wake up for you any time." Taking her package, he set it down on the table and took her into his arms in one motion. Jimmy's unshaven face bit into her soft skin, but she reveled in the mannish smell and feel of his body, responding to his kisses with passionate yearning.

Jimmy finally relaxed his embrace. Looking down into her face lovingly, he said, "You know, you really shouldn't be here. People can see your horse from the Pecos Road or from Indian Creek Road."

"I don't care," Grace said. "I'm going to be here all the time pretty soon."

"Now, you know we agreed with your father to wait a while," Jimmy said quickly. "I haven't got started on that room yet."

Grace ignored his words and turned toward the table. "Here's some fresh bread I helped make."

"Fresh bread?" Jimmy said. "You made fresh bread?"

"I helped make it," she repeated. "And I caught a fish, too."

"Well, aren't you the talented one," Jimmy said as he took the bread out of the sack and smelled it. "Hey, I can't wait." He quickly unwrapped the loaf, took a sharp knife from a drawer, cut a slice off the end, and took a big bite.

"Wait, I've got some jam here, too," Grace said.

"I'm sorry," Jimmy said. "I couldn't wait. This bread is just like my mother used to make. It's going to be a happy day when you're making it for me all the time. Sit down and I'll get some milk from my cooler, and we'll have a snack."

Jimmy walked out the back door and came back with a bottle of rich milk from the dairy. He shook the milk to mix the cream that had gathered at the top and poured two large glasses. Then he cut two thick slices of bread and covered them with jam, handing one to Grace. "Here darlin', is a treat fit for the queen of the Pecos. To the best little cook in the world," Jimmy said, saluting his bride-to-be.

Grace looked a little embarrassed. "I didn't really make that bread. Adele did, but I helped her. And I think I know how to do it myself now."

"Good," Jimmy said, pleased. "It'll be better than anything we had at the fiesta."

His mention of the fiesta brought a question to Grace's mind she had been wondering about. As she swallowed her last bite of bread, she took a long drink of cold milk and asked, "Who was the man you and Shoney seemed unhappy with at the dance? Remember, he had asked Vonnie to dance, and Shoney told him to stay away from her."

Jimmy cut himself another piece of bread and looked up, answering slowly. "I think you're talking about Bill McKane. He's a new guy in town, and we've seen him talking to the miners. We think he's trying to cause trouble. After he talks to the workers, they seem moody and uncooperative.

"What do you think is going to happen?" Grace asked cautiously.

"Nothing for you to worry about, my pretty one. We'll deal with McKane. Now I'm going to put this bread away and finish it later. And I think it's best for you to head home. Your dad may be worrying about you."

"I suppose," Grace said, as she reluctantly stood up.

Outside, Jimmy patted the horse's neck, gave Grace a quick kiss, and helped her into the saddle. "Thanks for the bread and jam. Next time you come, you can help me with that room," he said with a wink. "You might as well learn to be a carpenter as well as a cook."

"Not on your life," she threw back over her shoulder as she galloped off.

Grace slowed Dutch to a walk when she reached the Pecos Road, and upon approaching the Ponderosa Lodge, she was surprised to see her dad's Studebaker. I might as well ride over and see if my dad is there, she thought.

No one was in the dining room except Leota and her father, sitting at a far table by the window overlooking the river. They seemed to be talking about something important. Grace stood for a moment curiously watching the couple. She finally walked toward their table, and John Shockey raised his head and noticed her approaching. For an uncomfortable moment they stared at each other, neither of them sure what to say or do. Finally, John rose from the table and motioned Grace to come over. She hesitantly walked the last steps to the table and wondered why she felt like an intruder. Afterall, he is my father, she reminded herself.

"Hello, Grace," John said a little too brightly. "You must be on your way home. Would you like to join us for supper?"

He said 'us', not 'me', Grace noted to herself.

"No, thanks," Grace said quickly. "I'm not hungry. I had some fresh bread and jam that Adele made. I thought I'd just say hello and go on home."

"Whatever you wish, dear," John said in a relieved voice, Grace thought. "Leota and I have things to talk about."

"See you tomorrow," Leota said in a tone seeming to dismiss Grace.

Grace turned, tears stinging her eyes. "See you all later," she mumbled, heading for the door.

Duchess felt like an old friend as she climbed on her back. She rode the few miles home in a state of shock. This was the first woman she had seen her father interested in since her mother died. "This can't be," she kept murmuring over and over. "Not Leota Stevenson."

Tears rolled slowly down her cheeks and dropped on her saddle horn. She moved forward and laid her wet cheek on Duchess' neck. "Oh Mama, why did you have to go away?" Grace cried, feeling the pain of her loss all over again.

Instinctively, Duchess knew she must take care of her little mistress. She turned onto Holy Ghost Road without a signal from Grace and took the broken-hearted girl safely home. Grace stepped down from the saddle and faced the empty cabin. "So much for the good luck Mama's jelly was supposed to bring me," she said sadly. "It didn't quite last all day."

14

There was little conversation the next morning as Grace drove her father to work. He was preoccupied and didn't seem to notice that she drove faster than usual. The dust rose from the gravel road in a cloud, and pieces of rock hit the underside of the car with loud pings. *He's thinking of his dear Leota,* Grace thought and groaned inwardly.

When the impatient driver stopped in front of the mine office building, John gathered up his briefcase and jacket. Casting a last look at his daughter, he said, "Have a good day, dear. I'll be having dinner at the lodge after work, so I'll be late coming home."

"That's fine," Grace said stiffly. "I will be working in the restaurant after I close the shop. Leota asked me to help serve a special dinner tonight, but I didn't know you would be there."

"Yes," John said absently as he opened the door. "It's a mine management meeting. There are some important matters to discuss."

Well, I have an important matter to discuss with you, also, Mr. Shockey, Grace thought as she drove away. She tossed her hair back and looked straight ahead with smoldering eyes. *I want to know just what Leota Stevenson means to you.*

The gravel flew again, and the trees whizzed by as Grace headed to the lodge for her art class. She stamped into the room with hardly a glance at her teacher who stood over a sink cleaning brushes. Grace went directly to her easel and looked at her watercolor with a rueful eye. "I'm not getting any depth in my background," she grumbled. "These mountains look too close."

Vonnie Messier walked over to her disgruntled student. "Perspective problems? You need more shading here," she motioned with a pretty hand. "By the way, good morning, and how are you? Not so good, I assume."

Grace turned with a sigh, and the words tumbled out. "Oh Vonnie, I think my dad is interested in Leota. Have you heard any gossip?"

Vonnie put her arms around her student and friend. "No, I haven't, Grace. But your father is a very handsome man, and an eligible man. Leota is a pretty, unmarried widow, so I'm not surprised they've noticed each other."

"I saw them in the restaurant last night," Grace persisted. "Their heads were mighty close together, and they looked completely absorbed with each other."

Vonnie laughed. "What were you doing here last night? I doubt you were putting in extra time on your painting."

Grace moved back from her teacher's embrace. "I...I...I was coming back from visiting Adele," she said defensively.

Vonnie gently took one of Grace's hands. "Is Adele the only person you visited?"

"I stopped by Jimmy's, too. I took him some homemade bread. I didn't stay long." The words came tumbling out.

"Does your dad know?" Vonnie asked softly.

"No, he doesn't have to know everything," Grace said defiantly. "I'm nineteen years old, and I'm not a baby anymore."

"No, you're definitely not a baby," Vonnie agreed. "And how old is your father?"

Grace hesitated, and Vonnie patted her hand. "If you don't have to answer to him, he definitely doesn't have to answer to you."

Grace opened her mouth to protest but thought better of it. Vonnie patted her hand again. "Now help me get these brushes cleaned up."

The class went well after its rocky start. Grace became absorbed in her work, a view from their cabin on Holy Ghost Creek, which she had sketched one balmy fall evening. Golden leafed aspen trees shaded the water, and tall pines marched up the rugged mountain in the background. She worked on the shadows, trying to get the right distance between the creek and the mountain. Her negative feelings were quickly drowned as a creative mood began to monopolize her thoughts.

Just before lunch, Vonnie stepped back and looked at the almost completed picture. "You got it! You're getting the idea of how to portray depth and distance. That's very good. Some students never learn this technique."

"Do you really think I've got it right?"

"You might work a little more on the angle of this shadow in the water from this tree," Vonnie said, pointing to one of the aspen trees.

Grace looked over at the clock. "I'll do that tomorrow. I've got to get lunch because I go to work at one o'clock in the restaurant. I'm not working in the gift shop today. I have to prepare salads for a dinner tonight." Grace gave Vonnie a smile as she hurried out the door. "Thanks for listening."

🐦 🐦 🐦

After Grace finished the fruit salad that would be served with the roast beef dinner, she set the table, placing a white napkin beside each setting and put silverware in the correct position. She then arranged a centerpiece from pansies and violets and a few sprigs of currant twigs laden with red berries. The plants grew beside the back porch and were protected from the frosty winds which were just starting to herald the coming of winter. When she had finished, she stood back and admired her handiwork.

Just then Adele walked by and gave the table an approving look. "Nice," she said.

Grace suddenly heard Leota's heels clicking behind her. Her boss carefully surveyed the table. "Good job, Grace. I like the colors in your arrangement."

"Thank you," an unsmiling Grace managed to say.

"Now you can put your salads on and fill the water glasses," Leota directed. "The men will be here soon. You and Adele will serve this table. If other customers come in, let Adele take them, and you work on this dinner party. Once you get the food served, all you have to do is watch the drinks and refill them. When it's time for dessert, Adele or I will help you."

"Yes ma'am," Grace said quietly. She was beginning to feel a little excited about serving dinner. It would be a new experience, and she had always thrived on "adventures," as she called them. It kept life from getting boring. I just hope I don't pour hot coffee in someone's lap, she thought.

The dinner party soon trooped in, and Leota went to greet them. Grace spotted her father, the mine president, Mark Mattson, the superintendent, Ted Cooper, and Shoney Terrell, a shift boss, among the group. She felt very important as she swished back and forth between their table and the kitchen.

The busy server was just removing plates so the dessert could be served when her father announced, "I want everyone to know that this lovely young lady is my daughter, Grace." Grace blushed, and they gave her a round of applause. She smiled broadly, but lingered only a moment before heading back to the kitchen.

"She's a beauty, John," Grace heard as she left the dining room. "You'll have to keep an eye on her," someone said above a loud burst of laughter.

Too late, she thought. And besides, I'm the one who should be keeping an eye on you, Dad.

Leota quickly helped Grace place the apple cobbler on a tray to serve the dessert. Sure, Grace thought as a frown creased her smooth forehead. She just wants to serve my dad his dessert.

Before returning to the kitchen, Leota made an announcement. "The Joe Louis, Max Baer prize fight will be on the radio in a few minutes. Feel free to stay here as long as you want to discuss your business and listen to the fight. Grace will be happy to continue serving coffee for your enjoyment."

Grace filled their cups and went over to the counter with Adele. "Well, I got that done without too much trouble. Do you need any help?"

"Nope," Adele said as she wiped the counter. "Things are purty quiet right now."

"Who are those other men at that table?" Grace asked.

"The two Spanish men are shift bosses," Adele replied. "I'm not sure what their names are. The other men are big shots from the head office of the American Metal Comp'ny. They must be checkin' up on how things are goin' at the mine."

"What do you suppose they're concerned about?" Grace asked. "I heard one of them say that the miners are getting upset."

"There's a union organizer here in town tryin' to sign up the miners," Adele said. "They're prob'ly talkin' about how to keep the union out."

"How do you know this?" Grace asked with a puzzled expression on her face. "My dad hasn't mentioned anything to me; neither has Jimmy."

"Eric told me," Adele said. "He don't like the idea of the union. He says there is goin' to be big trouble."

"I don't know anything about unions," Grace said. "Why would the miners want to join a union?"

"The union promises to get 'em better wages," Adele replied, "but Eric feels he's darn lucky to have a job durin' this Depression. He says there are many people out o' work in the country, and we have a steady payroll here, so we should 'preciate it."

"I'll have to talk to Dad and Jimmy about this," Grace said quietly as she went to serve fresh coffee.

Grace soon came back and placed the coffee pot on a warmer. "That should do it for a while," she said to Adele.

Just then Leota walked over to the radio behind the counter and turned it on. "Welcome, ladies and gentlemen," came the deep voice of an announcer, "to the heavy weight championship fight. Pretty boy, Max Baer, takes on the Brown Bomber, Joe Louis, in a twelve round battle."

As the men settled down to listen to the fight, Adele and Grace grabbed a couple of stools to rest their feet. They sat in silence for a few minutes while the announcer droned on, and then a bell clanged when the fight started. Neither girl was interested, and they soon began whispering. "Do you have a dress I could borry fer next weekend?" Adele asked.

Grace looked curiously at her friend. "Sure. What do you want it for?"

"I'm takin' work off on Friday. Eric and I are goin' to Santa Fe."

"Oh?" Grace said, her eyes large.

"Yeah," Adele said. "Eric and me, well, we are goin' to git married."

"What?" Grace said loudly, getting up from her stool.

Leota stuck her head out from the kitchen and gave a stern "Shush!"

"I'm sorry," Grace said and hurried to refill the coffee cups.

Coming back to the counter, Grace stared directly at her friend. "What did you say?"

"You heered me. Me and Eric is goin' to get hitched, an' I don't have a dress-up dress."

"I've got a blue one that would look good on you," Grace said, peering at Adele in round-eyed surprise. "Why are you doing this?" she added lamely.

Adele looked thoughtful for a moment. "Well, I reckon I loves him."

"Well, I hope so," Grace said shaking her head in disbelief.

"I told Leota today I'm quittin' after Thursday," Adele said.

"Well, I'm going to miss you," Grace replied.

"We'll see each other sometimes," Adele said. "The Andersons' house is up in Gifford Town. You can come up an' visit me once in a while, an' I'll give you cookin' lessons. Yore goin' to need 'em, you know."

Adele looked at Grace with a teasing smile, and Grace poked her with her elbow. "Well, I hope you like to cook, with all those men you'll be feeding."

"I know," Adele replied with a smile.

The girls were quiet as the radio blared out a count, "...eight, nine, ten, and he's out. The winner by a knockout, Joe Louis!" A roar of approval filled the room.

Just as Grace reached for the coffee pot, she noticed a man entering the room attired in a black suit with a bright red tie.

"Well, looky here," he said to those seated around the table. "All the mighty mucks of the mine. Can I join you gentlemen?"

Grace looked over at Shoney who was sitting at the end of the table. The big man rose quickly and pointed his finger at the intruder. "The answer to that question is NO, and you know why."

The man in the dark suit stared over at Shoney. "Well, Mr. Terrell, you have advanced to a point where you are speaking for the president of the company?"

Mark Mattson bolted out of his seat. "Mr. Terrell is speaking for everyone at this table, Bill McKane. You are not welcome here."

McKane's eyes swept around the table. "All right, gentlemen. It's obvious you're all company men, so I'm sure I'm not wanted. But the time will come when you'll all have to talk to me. And, Terrell, for sure you and I will be talking later."

"I got nothin' to talk to you about, rabble rouser," Shoney snarled.

Bill McKane's face turned deep red, as he clenched his fists. "We'll see about that Terrell. You think you're pretty tough bcause you whipped a few punks in the Army. Do you think you can take me, Company Man?"

Shoney made a swift move toward McKane, but Ted Cooper and one of the others grabbed his arms. "Get out of here, McKane," Ted Cooper ordered. "You weren't invited here, and you are not welcome. Get out before we turn Shoney loose on you."

Bill McKane stood his ground for a few seconds and then turned to go. "We'll settle this later, Company Man," he sneered, glaring at Shoney through slitted eyes.

Grace had quietly taken refuge behind the counter and was relieved when the dinner group started to disband after Bill McKane went out the door. She listened carefully as Mark Mattson gave his last instructions. "I want daily reports, gentlemen, on the state of affairs. I'm afraid we've got big troubles."

Leota came out from the kitchen and joined the girls at the counter. John Shockey sauntered over as the others were leaving. "Thanks for a fine meal, Leota. Too bad everything else didn't turn out as well as the food."

Grace noticed Leota's eyes as she returned her father's gaze, and couldn't help but detect the tenderness in her eyes. I'm right, she thought. I don't know if Dad knows it, but that woman is out to get him. But it's going to be over my dead body.

"Is it all right if I leave now, Leota?" Grace asked abruptly. "Dad needs a ride home."

"Sure," Leota replied easily. "Good job tonight, Grace. You handled that table like a pro."

"It wasn't that hard," Grace said curtly. "Come on, Dad, let's go. It's been a long day."

"So it has," John said as he smiled and saluted Leota and Adele. "Goodnight, ladies."

Grace looked back at Adele as she reached the door and gave her a wave and a nod to let her know she would bring her a dress. "Tomorrow," she mouthed the words.

"I'll drive," John said as they reached the car.

As Grace slid into her seat, she was suddenly aware of the nervous knot in her stomach and a premonition warning her that troubled days were surely ahead.

15

Grace spent a fitful night thinking about what had happened at the lodge. She couldn't reconcile herself to Adele's getting married. Does she know what she's doing? Is she really in love? These were the questions that kept going through her mind. And finally, she had another chilling thought. Do I know what I am doing? Am I really in love? It was all very confusing.

The fear about a relationship between Leota and her father was just as upsetting. Her intuition told her something was going on there, and she was bewildered as to how to cope with this troubling possibility. Her mind went back to what Vonnie had said. She was clearly trying to tell her to stay out of her father's personal life. But he's my dad, and it's my business what he does, she kept telling herself as she tossed and turned in frustration.

Along with all her troubled thoughts, Bill McKane's image kept intruding as well. She could not dismiss the big man with his slick black hair and his threatening sneer. Who is he? And why does he bother me so much? These were questions that kept running through her head.

"There's so much I don't understand right now," she whispered to herself before she finally drifted off into an uneasy sleep.

The next morning Grace walked through the door of the lodge and headed directly toward the counter where Adele was waiting on a customer. She placed a paper sack in front of her friend and whispered, "Here's what you wanted."

Adele barely glanced in her direction as she poured coffee. "Thanks," was all she said.

Grace then hurried down the hall to the art room. Vonnie was at her desk and greeted her with a smile. "How are things this morning?" she asked brightly.

"I couldn't sleep much last night."

"You do look a little tired."

Grace rubbed her eyes and then blurted out, "Adele is getting married."

"Really?" Vonnie asked, surprise in her voice. "I didn't know she was seeing anyone."

"Remember the fellow at the fiesta dance? Eric Anderson. They've been writing to each other. I don't know how much they've actually been together."

"I understand your concern." Vonnie tapped her pencil on the desk, turning this information over in her mind. "Well, Adele is a pretty sensible girl," she said, finally. "She probably knows what she's doing." Then in a lighter tone she continued, "You are a good friend to worry about her. But I'm worried about you. How are things going? Are you possibly having second thoughts about yourself?" Vonnie's dark eyes showed concern as she looked straight into Grace's anxious gray eyes.

She's so smart, Grace thought. She knows I'm not just worried about Adele. "Never," she said in a firm voice.

"Is there anything else?" Vonnie asked softly.

A frown appeared on Grace's forehead. "Do you remember that fellow in Santa Fe who wanted to dance with you, and Shoney and Jimmy didn't like it?" Vonnie nodded her head. "Well, he was at the lodge yesterday. There's something about him that scares me."

After a moment's thought, Vonnie said slowly, "You're talking about Bill McKane. Well, your perception is right. He's an outsider who has come in trying to organize the miners against the company. Actually, he's right in some ways. He's telling the miners they should have higher wages and better working conditions. This is true, but the tactics he's using are causing trouble. He's not a good negotiator for the miners. No progress has been made with the company, and the miners are starting to get rebellious."

"How do you know all this?" Grace asked.

"Shoney told me," Vonnie said, and then she smiled. "He's been to Santa Fe to see me a few times since the fiesta."

"Oh!" Grace said, surprised. "Something else I didn't know about. I can't believe everything that's going on."

"Well, now you know. I like that big handsome Shoney. He's a different kind of man than I knew in Paris." Vonnie's laugh tinkled like a silver bell, and her face flushed.

"I imagine so," Grace responded with a grin. "He's a little old, but I can see why you would like him." Vonnie's news had lifted her spirits.

"He's not old, and I do like him," Vonnie said, relieved at her student's lighter mood. "By the way, I have some good news for you. Mr. Mattson had breakfast here this morning, and he noticed your coyote picture and bought it."

Vonnie opened her desk drawer. "Twenty-five bucks, Miss Artist, after taking out a small framing fee. You have sold your first work of art."

Grace put out her hand tentatively. "He bought my picture?" she said slowly. "This is unbelievable."

"Not really," Vonnie said matter-of-factly. "It's a good picture, and you are going to sell many pictures, my dear. The talent is there, and you're going to use it. I'm very proud of you. This will also encourage the other students."

Grace was almost overwhelmed by this unexpected stroke of good luck. The president of the mining company, no less, had bought her picture. He would put it up on the wall of his beautiful home. Her own picture! Life was suddenly better, and she attacked her troubled watercolor with new enthusiasm.

Grace was just rearranging a shelf of pottery when Jimmy walked into the shop that afternoon. She was still in a rosy glow over her sale, and she ran to give him a hug, bumping into the counter. "Careful, Tex," he said. "Let's not destroy the property."

"Oh Jimmy, I sold a picture today!"

"Well, that's good news. I haven't seen you this excited in a long time."

"Not since you asked me to marry you," Grace said, looking deeply into his eyes.

"Not even then," Jimmy said with a grin.

Grace touched his face, and her fingers moved down to the sensitive lips she knew and loved so well. "Yes, even then, sweetheart. Don't you know you're the most important thing in the world to me?" As she said the words, Grace realized she was reaffirming her love for him and casting aside any doubts that had been plaguing her.

Jimmy looked down at this girl who had become so precious to him. "What would I do without you, darlin'?"

Grace stared into the serious brown eyes that seemed strangely preoccupied. "What is it, Jimmy? Is the mine situation getting to you?"

He smiled slightly. "How did you know? You are not only pretty; you're smart, too."

"Mr. Mattson and some of the bosses were here yesterday talking about things. What's going to happen, Jimmy?"

"There may be a strike," he said as he moved toward the window. "The miners are getting pretty riled up."

"What will you do?" Grace asked quietly.

"I'm pulled both ways. The miners should be given more consideration, but I don't like the way McKane is handling it."

Grace suddenly had an idea. "Why don't you get on the negotiating team? You could work for the miners better than he has."

"I've thought of that," Jimmy said tiredly, "but I don't think Shoney would like it too much."

"Talk to him and make him understand," Grace persisted. "You're a good communicator." She put her arms around his waist and hugged him tightly.

Jimmy smiled down into the eyes of this girl who understood him so well. "What would I ever do without you, Tex? Don't let Vonnie put any notions into your head about going to Paris to study art."

"Where did you get that idea?" Grace exclaimed. "And leave the Pecos? Don't you ever believe such a thing."

"Promise?"

"I promise, and I'll seal it with a kiss."

Grace turned her smiling face up to Jimmy for a kiss just as Leota came through the door. "Excuse me," she said, "but I need to talk to you, Grace."

Jimmy looked embarrassed and headed for the door. "I've got to go. Hello, Mrs. Stevenson."

Leota smiled. "Hello Jimmy. You don't have to go. You need to hear what I'm going to say, too."

"Yes, ma'am." Jimmy paused in the doorway and looked questioningly at Leota.

"I'm thinking we should have a party for Adele and Eric on Saturday night to celebrate their wedding. I can close the dining room at nine o'clock and move the tables back, and we can have a dance. What do you think of that?"

"That's wonderful!" Grace said.

"And here's where you can help us, Jimmy. You can spread the news to Eric's friends that they're invited."

"Sure, I'll do that," Jimmy said. "I'll even post a notice on the bulletin board in the Dryhouse."

"Fine. Then it's settled," Leota said as she left.

"Looks like I've got a shivaree to plan," Jimmy said with a mischievous smile.

"Don't be too mean," Grace warned.

"No meaner than they'll be to us when we get married," Jimmy said with a grin.

Grace watched Jimmy's long-legged strides as he headed down the hall. How could I ever doubt for a minute that you are my destiny, Jimmy Kirkwood? She frowned at her misgivings and went back into the shop to help a customer who had just walked in and was looking at the Indian pottery.

Would you be interested in this Indian wedding vase?" Grace asked sweetly as she held up the special piece she had created. "I made it myself."

She won't like it. It's not as good as the rest of the pottery, Grace thought. That's all right. I'll use it at my own wedding.

16

The next few days went swiftly as mine officials negotiated with McKane and a team of miners for better salaries and working conditions, but no agreement was reached. A feeling of impending doom hung over the mining town as actual winter storm clouds gathered over the Pecos Canyon. Men gathered in groups at the store and the post office, exchanging information and shaking their heads at the lack of good news. Women met in homes and drank coffee and felt their nerves tightening at the thought of no pay checks for an indefinite period of time. Suspicion carved wedges between friends as some miners leaned toward striking, and others said they would cross the strike lines and work. The carefree times of summer, when the mining town's biggest worry had been winning the state baseball championship, were buried in the hateful emotions of men at secret meetings baring their souls because of their distrust and resentment of "The Company."

"They are getting richer while you work your lives away like dogs," Bill McKane pounded into receptive ears at each meeting. He set a night to have all the miners vote on the strike if an agreement weren't reached soon.

The foreboding events at the mine were affecting the atmosphere at the Ponderosa Lodge as well. Business dropped off as men worried about the basic needs of a job and money. Leota was concerned not only for her business, but for John Shockey, who was taking a strong stand against the organized men. She had lived in a mining town long enough to know the current divisive situation could lead to violence, and company loyalists were often the targets of frenzied union men.

Adele said nothing, but she knew Eric could be in danger because of his stand to keep on working. And she also was certain her strong minded Swedish husband-to-be would never retreat a step because of any threat from the strike sympathizers.

Grace stopped driving her father to work because he was concerned for her safety. Ted Cooper picked him up every morning.

Jimmy said very little to Grace about the conflict, but she could feel the stress in his looks and his touch, and she was seeing little of him these days. He seemed to be busier than usual, and he appeared to have the weight of the world on his shoulders.

"How is everything going?" Grace asked Jimmy one day when he dropped by the gift shop.

He shrugged his shoulders. "Your guess is as good as mine."

Grace looked him directly in the eyes and sighed in frustration. "You don't tell me anything."

Jimmy returned her look and then averted his eyes. "See you later," he said as he turned to go.

"Oh blast!" Grace exploded. "Don't tell me, then. See if I care." Jimmy beat a hasty retreat down the hall.

Shortly after this unpleasant exchange, Leota and a stranger came in while Grace was standing at the counter reading an article on Indian pottery. She put the brochure aside and glanced up at her boss for a moment, then shifted her attention to Leota's companion. My goodness! she thought. What a handsome man! Her smokey gray eyes hardly flickered, however, as she looked cooly at the newcomer.

"Grace, this is Bradley Thornton from Hollywood, California. He is staying in one of our cabins for a few days. Bradley, this is Grace Shockey. She's on our staff and manages this gift shop, among other things."

Bradley Thornton was a tall man with dark wavy hair combed back from his forehead. His blue eyes were framed with thick dark lashes. A long straight nose, a full sensual mouth, and a strong chin completed the picture of the most striking looking man Grace had ever seen. He looks like a movie star, and maybe he is one since he's from Hollywood, she thought.

Even though she was bubbling with excitement on the inside, however, Grace maintained her outward composure. "Hello," she said formally. Her full lips broke into a smile, and the lashes over her gray eyes fluttered briefly.

The California gentleman came forward and took her limp hand in a warm strong clasp. His eyes looked straight into her wide expressionless ones, and Grace felt her heart jump wildly as she almost gasped audibly for air. "Nice to meet you," she managed to say.

"The pleasure is all mine," her new acquaintance replied in a deep warm voice that could have melted the ice on the Pecos in the middle of winter.

"I've invited Bradley to our party for Adele and Eric," Leota said, breaking the electric silence crackling in the air. "Bradley would like to get acquainted with some of the local people while he's here. Who knows, maybe he'll put us all in a movie someday." Leota looked up at her attractive guest with unabashed pleasure.

Bradley reluctantly tore his eyes from Grace and turned to Leota. "Actually, I am here on movie business," he said. "I'll be looking over one of your local girls with the hope that I can sign her to a movie contract. I'll also just be enjoying a few days vacation in this beautiful country. I've never seen such breathtaking scenery."

Grace's paralyzed tongue suddenly came to life. "You've come to the right place, Mr. Thornton. If you need a guide to help you enjoy your days, I'll be glad to help you." Her eyes were sparkling as she directed a glittering smile toward the Hollywood visitor. She had forgotten her very busy schedule for the moment.

"Oh yes," Leota said with a wave of her hand. "Grace would be an excellent guide. She's an ardent horsewoman, along with being a good sales clerk and a superb artist. I guess about the only thing she can't do is cook, and she's working on that."

Ignoring that last remark, Grace turned her attention to Bradley and said in her sweetest tone, "Welcome to the Ponderosa, Mr. Thornton. You will enjoy our party Saturday night. We'll show you how we celebrate on the Pecos."

"I'll look forward to seeing you again," Bradley said smoothly as Leota took his arm and started for the door.

Grace sat down weakly on one of the stools in the gift shop. Her heart was still racing, and all the bad premonitions that had enveloped her over the last few days were gone. "For some reason, I feel better than I have in a long time," she murmured to herself. "Life is certainly going to be more interesting around this place now."

She suddenly thought of her scrapbook at home in her bedroom. She had been collecting pictures of movie stars since she was a little girl and pasting them in this book. I don't have one picture that looks better than Mr. Thornton, she thought. He resembles Robert Taylor. What is someone who looks like that doing staying in the Ponderosa Lodge?

Then the picture of Jimmy crept into her rosy reflections. She was immediately overwhelmed with guilt as she thought of her reaction to this new man. You're going to marry Jimmy, remember? she reprimanded herself sternly. Forget about Bradley Thornton from Hollywood.

But her thoughts kept straying, and a few minutes later as she reviewed her conversation with their intriguing guest, she recalled him saying that he was here to try to sign a local girl to a movie contract. That's kind of unbelievable, she reasoned. Who might that be? She couldn't bring to mind anyone whose looks would put her in a category to be a Hollywood star.

🍂 🍂 🍂

On Saturday night, an excited crowd gathered at the lodge to celebrate the wedding of Adele and Eric. Leota and John, Grace and Jimmy, and Vonnie and Shoney took a table together. They sipped coffee and ice tea and waited for the honored guests to return from Santa Fe.

Adele and Eric had planned to be married by a municipal judge on Friday and spend their first night in a small hotel. Vonnie had made reservations for them in one of the hotels near the Plaza, and had left word for them to stop by the lodge at nine o'clock Saturday night on their way home.

Jimmy looked around at the people who were seated in the dining room. "There's not too many here," he observed as he exchanged looks with Shoney. "I guess it's not a good time for parties right now," he concluded lamely.

"What do you mean?" Grace asked.

But before Jimmy could answer, Adele and Eric suddenly appeared in the doorway. A shower of rice rained down on the two amid laughter and well wishes as the newlyweds made their way into the room. Looking uncertain and embarrassed, they shook the rice from their hair and clothing.

Leota ran to greet the guests of honor. "Let's have a big hand for Mr. and Mrs. Eric Anderson," she called out. As cheers and whistles rocked the room, she led the couple to the table where Adele's parents and Eric's brothers were sitting. They seemed relieved to be surrounded by familiar faces, but Adele still appeared stiff in her borrowed blue dress, and Eric looked uncomfortable in his tight suit and short haircut.

"Music," Leota commanded with a wave of her hand, and the fiddler, guitarist, and accordian player burst into the opening notes of, "Here Comes the Bride." The musicians played only a few bars of the traditional wedding song and then switched to the popular waltz, "Let the Rest of the World Go By."

"We'll build a sweet little nest, somewhere in the west, and let the rest of the world go by," the guitar player sang softly to the accompaniment of the music.

Everyone was waiting for Adele and Eric to begin the first dance, but they just sat uncertainly at their table. Leota quickly went over and whispered to them, and they reluctantly started toward the floor. Everyone clapped, and then other partners joined in the dance as the merriment began.

A short time later, Grace and Jimmy were dancing to the "Beer Barrel Polka" when out of the corner of her eye, Grace spotted Bradley Thornton leaning against the counter at the other end of the room. Her heart skipped a beat even though her feet kept in time, and she said breathlessly, "He's here."

"Who's here?" Jimmy asked, looking around the room.

Grace just smiled and shook her head. "Nobody."

Returning to their table after the dance, Jimmy asked Grace if she would like a drink. "Lemonade," Grace replied, smiling over at him. Jimmy turned and left as Grace leaned back in her chair. My feet hurt, she thought, looking down at her high heels. She had found a pretty pair of red pumps to match her red dress in her mother's closet. Darn uncomfortable shoes, she thought.

Grace's eyes wandered over to where her father and Leota were dancing. You can tell to look at her she thinks she's in heaven dancing with my dad, she thought sourly.

Suddenly, Vonnie and Shoney danced by with a swish of skirts and a tapping of toes. The big man was smoothly leading his little dark haired partner around the room in perfect rhythm and movement. What a pair they make, Grace thought. He's so big and good looking, and she's so petite and pretty. Grace could see the love and pride in Vonnie's eyes as she waved and then looked adoringly up at her partner.

By now Adele and Eric had given up on dancing. They looked tired, but exhilarated. That blue dress does her more justice than it did me, Grace thought as she looked over at Adele. Grace remembered wearing the dress to her mother's funeral. She had told Adele she could keep it. She knew she would never wear it again, and realistically, Grace knew Adele would probably not be able to afford a dress like that for a long time. So she could have it, and welcome to it.

Grace then decided it was time to say a few words to the happy couple, but just as she got up from her table someone tapped her on the elbow.

"Could I have this dance?" Bradley Thornton asked graciously.

"Well, I was just...well, I guess...well, yes, Mr. Thornton."

"Brad, please," he said in a soft voice.

Grace felt awkward as she went into Brad's arms, but that passed quickly as their steps blended as naturally as if they had always been dancing partners. She felt Brad's arm tighten around her waist, and she blissfully leaned her head on his shoulder.

"You're a wonderful dancer, Grace. I can't believe I'm dancing with such a gorgeous girl in this lovely spot on the Pecos. You're definitely a fantasy come true. I must tell you, I've always dreamed of a girl like you."

Grace basked in the hypnotism of her partner's melodious voice until she suddenly came back to reality. Quickly pulling her head back, she looked up at him sharply. "You don't really know what kind of girl I am just because you like the way I dance," she remarked defensively.

"You are so right, my dear. All the more reason for me to get to know you better," Brad said, looking down at the girl in his arms with a teasing smile.

"Well, I'm pretty busy," Grace said quickly. "I have art classes in the mornings, and I work in the afternoons."

"I'm going to speak to your boss," Brad said. "She must let you off one afternoon so we can go for a horseback ride and maybe do a little fishing. Would you like that?"

"Of course," Grace said without thinking as she looked, spellbound, into his amazing blue eyes.

"Tag dance," someone shouted, and suddenly Jimmy appeared, pulling her away from her dream world into the reality of his strong arms.

"Who is Fancy Boy?" he growled.

"Do you mean Bradley Thornton?" Grace replied, trying to look innocent.

"What's he doing here?"

"He's staying in one of the cabins. Leota introduced him to me today. He says he's here to try to get someone to sign a movie contract."

"Who?" Jimmy asked, suspicion in his voice.

"I don't know," Grace said truthfully. "I think I'll ask him that tonight."

"Let's go get some food," Jimmy said abruptly. "I'm starved."

They filled their plates and sat down in an awkward silence. Finally Grace said in a slightly strained voice, "This is the best food I've ever eaten." Jimmy looked at her with perplexed brown eyes.

Suddenly all eyes turned to the front door as it slammed with a loud bang. And there stood Bill McKane, stocky legs spread apart, his muscled arms on his hips. He broke the silence that instantly filled the room with words he flung from his mouth like a shot. "I just thought you'd like to know the news. The miners voted to strike tonight, so they won't be on the job Monday."

Eric jumped to his feet, reaching McKane with a few long steps. "I 'ust want you to know, Mister, I will be at work on Monday, as usual, ya." Eric stared down at the husky man from his superior height. The strong set of his shoulders and intense look in his Scandinavian blue eyes left no doubt about the meaning of his words.

"That's your choice, Swede boy. But not a wise one. In fact, I think it's pretty stupid."

Eric clenched his fists and made a move toward McKane, but Shoney sprang to his side, holding his arms. "Steady, Eric. He's not worth it." Raising his voice, he thundered, "Get the hell out of here, Bill McKane."

The uninvited guest turned and hastily made an exit. "We'll settle this later, Terrell," were the threatening words flung over his shoulder.

Shoney whispered quickly into Eric's ear and then walked swiftly back to Vonnie. "I'll be gone a while, Von. Just stay here. I'll be back for you a little later." Shoney's eyes then focused on Jimmy, and he gave him a silent signal with a nod of his head. Shoney, Eric, and Jimmy quickly walked across the room and out the door without another word.

The shocked wedding guests were brought back to reality when the musicians suddenly started playing a lively tune, "Turkey in the Straw." A few couples slowly got up and tried to dance away their fears of the impending strike, but most sat as if in a trance.

Grace sat quietly with her eyes glued on the door that had closed behind Jimmy and the other men. Suddenly Vonnie nudged her and said under her breath, "Here comes Mr. Wonderful."

Brad bowed low before Grace and said in a deep voice, "I would like to try this one with you."

Grace slowly rose like a wooden doll and followed Brad onto the dance floor. But when he turned to take her in his arms, her voice faltered. "I don't think I can dance now after what has happened. I'm sorry."

"That's all right," Brad replied easily. "I probably can't dance to that fast music anyway. Is there some place where we can just sit down and visit? Some place away from the people and the music."

Grace nodded and led Brad down the hall to the gift shop. She unlocked it, turned the light on, and shut the door.

"Sit down," Brad said, concern in his voice. "This strike must be bad news."

"We've been worried this would happen for some time, and now it's a reality. Yes, this is very bad news," Grace said slowly.

They sat quietly for a few moments. "Grace, tell me about yourself," Brad finally said. "You know about me. I'm a movie scout, and I'm here to offer Fabiola Manteau a contract. Do you know this girl?"

"So that's who you are after," Grace said with a smile. "Of course, I know Fabiola. She graduated with me from high school, but I haven't seen her for a long time."

"She goes to college in Santa Fe," Brad said. "She was in a beauty pageant there and won Miss Santa Fe. Last week she also won the Miss New Mexico crown in Albuquerque. One of our movie scouts spotted her and recommended we sign her up. I'm here to try to make a deal with her parents. They aren't too keen on the idea of her going to California. She's a beautiful talented girl, and I know she could have a successful career in Hollywood."

"I'm sure she would," Grace agreed. "She is so smart and so pretty. She's part French, you know."

"Yes," Brad said. "That French and Spanish mixture is dynamite." He looked intently at Grace. "You're quite attractive yourself, you know."

"Well, don't talk to me about Hollywood," Grace said with a laugh. "I'm a New Mexico convert. I'll never leave the Pecos."

"Lucky New Mexico," he replied. Then he added as he looked into a glass case, "Show me some of your Indian jewelry. I've never seen anything like this before."

As Grace displayed her merchandise, she talked about the legends she had picked up from the Indian suppliers, and her worries about the strike were pushed to the back of her mind.

"I must tell you about this Indian Wedding Vase," she said, smiling as she turned toward the pottery shelf.

"It's so good to see that gorgeous smile again," Brad said sincerely. "But let's save that story for another time. I need to get to my cabin and turn in since I have an early appointment with Mrs. Manteau. Do you feel better now?" Brad asked, looking tenderly into Grace's eyes.

"Yes, I do," Grace said softly. "Thanks for taking the time to help me get control of myself."

"Anytime," Brad said as he opened the door for them to return to the dance. "Hm-m, very interesting. Not only have I found a beauty queen, but also a Pecos queen. Is that what they call you?"

Grace laughed and closed the door. "How did you know?"

Brad took her arm and led her down the hall. "I know many things, my pretty one, and it's going to be fun teaching you some of them."

Grace walked dreamily back to her table. Brad smiled and held her chair as she sat down. She felt like royalty. "I guess I really am the Pecos Queen," she murmured, unaware of the curious looks from Leota and Vonnie.

"Shoney and the boys have gone to check on McKane's activities tonight. They don't trust him," Vonnie explained. "The shivaree is off as well."

The words sailed meaninglessly over Grace's head. She had forgotten the strike and the wedding. Her eyes and heart followed the retreating broad shoulders of Bradley Thornton.

17

The first week of the strike passed in threatening silence. Lines of miners gathered at the bottom of the hill and glared sullenly at the few men who climbed the stairs to their jobs. Those workers glanced uneasily at the faces of former friends as they hurried by. Women stayed inside, not understanding everything that was happening, but consumed with overpowering aching anxiety.

Grace continued her art class and work in the gift shop. She saw little of Jimmy. He wasn't working, but he seemed to be very busy anyway. She knew he had struggled with the decision to go out with the strikers. Her father was very unhappy with him, and she was again having serious questions about their relationship. This whole idea of refusing to work to achieve your demands was a totally foreign concept to her. Her father had always worked every day on the farm whether he was going to make any money on his crop or not. And he still continued to go to his office every morning at the mine.

Besides being worried about Jimmy's going out with the strikers, Grace was more concerned that she wasn't seeing much of him these days. When he did stop by the lodge for a quick visit, he seemed preoccupied and reluctant to talk to her. He acts so distant, she thought. His mind is on everything but me.

It didn't help to have her dad remind her often that he had been right to ask them to wait a year before getting married. And, when later in the week John told her about being called a "scab" and having rocks hurled at him as he ducked into the office door, Grace found herself on the defensive for Jimmy and seriously concerned for the welfare of her father, at the same time.

"They are threatening to burn down the homes of the men who don't join in the strike," John told her later. "Since we're gone all day long, I worry about our cabin. I've asked Ted Cooper to have a regular patrol check our place. The company is hiring security people to guard the mine and make periodic checks of the homes of the men continuing to work. Violence could break out any time, so the sheriff's office in Las Vegas is considering sending extra deputies up to this area."

Grace wanted to see Jimmy and talk to him about everything. But one day when he didn't stop by, she walked up to his cabin after she got out of art class. He wasn't there, and she sat down on a wooden bench near the woodpile. Just being near the place where he chopped wood made her feel a little closer to him.

Grace then slowly leaned over, resting her head in her hands. "Oh Jimmy," she sobbed. "I'm so confused about everything. I don't understand what is going on at the mine, and I don't understand what is going on with us."

The tears streamed down her cold cheeks, and she let them flow in unrestrained misery. She couldn't allow her father to see her anxiety at home, and she tried to keep her mind off her troubles when she was at the lodge. Things had bottled up inside her, and the release felt good.

Finally she got control of herself and wiped her face with the sleeves of her jacket. No handkerchief, she thought to herself. Mama always used to say I never had a hankie when I needed one. Thinking of her mother brought fresh tears. If she had ever needed her mother, it was now. But she also knew she would have to figure out things for herself.

Grace shook the tears away again and looked up at the sky. The serene view above her head reminded her of something else her mother had often said, "God's in His heaven; all's well with the world."

"I don't know, Mama," she said aloud. "I just don't know."

Grace suddenly noticed the ore cars moving silently across the sky over Indian Creek Canyon. The company had built a tramway from the mine to Alamitos, near Pecos, to transport the ore to the mill there. Her father had told her it was the longest aerial tramway on the North American continent. She wished she could be in one of those cars and glide away from all her worries. "What an experience it would be to ride that tramway!" she said to a squirrel clinging to the side of a pine tree and looking inquiringly at her with bright eyes.

The thought of riding the tramway chased away her depression for the moment, and she walked around the house to check on the room Jimmy was building. He had the roof and outside walls finished. Grace went inside the pine board structure and looked out the hole in the wall he had left for a window. She turned toward the corner where the bed would be. She felt her chilled body warmed by the thought of lying there with Jimmy. Then everything will be all right, she thought with a half-hearted smile.

Grace suddenly realized she must hurry back to the lodge to open the gift shop. A few minutes after arriving, Leota poked her head in. "Glad to see you're here. I was wondering if you were going to open up this afternoon," she said with forced cheerfulness.

Grace offered her a pained smile and began going through the mail. I don't really feel like talking to you, she thought as she slapped a bill down on the counter. I know I have to be nice to you. "But not today," she said aloud as Leota's quick footsteps echoed down the hall.

Suddenly, Grace looked up to see Bradley Thornton materialize in the room in all his breaktaking good looks. Her spirits rose instantly, and she smiled her first sincere smile of the day. "Hello Brad. And what can I do for you?"

Brad stood in front of the counter and looked at her a long moment with warm friendly eyes. He leaned toward her and gave her a dazzling smile. "I have an idea for us."

"Oh, I'm busy," Grace said quickly, not daring to ask what he had in mind.

"You're busy now," Brad said. "But you won't be busy on Sunday. How about showing me the sights of Tererro on Sunday afternoon? Then we'll have dinner in the little restaurant there. I think it would be fun to eat some Mexican food."

"Well," Grace said slowly, her instincts telling her that Jimmy wouldn't like this at all. But then, she wasn't seeing Jimmy very much these days, and he certainly wasn't going to take her anywhere on Sunday.

"Come on," Brad pleaded. "I won't be here much longer, and I'd like to explore this unique place."

"Well..." Grace said hesitantly.

"I'll get a horse from the lodge," Brad interrupted. "I know you like to ride, and we could head up the Pecos."

Brad's eyes were eloquent as they pleaded for an affirmative answer, and Grace's inhibitions suddenly flew out the window. "I'll meet you at the Holy Ghost turnoff about one o'clock on Sunday afternoon," she said with a smile that matched his.

"Wonderful," Brad said, turning quickly to leave as if fearing she might change her mind if he lingered. "I'm going to talk to Mr. and Mrs. Manteau this afternoon. He's not working today because of the strike. It looks like I've convinced them to let me take Fabiola with me when I leave."

Grace stood like a statue after Brad vanished. The thought of going for a ride with him and being taken to dinner was more than she could process at the moment. She just knew she felt good for the first time that day.

Then she thought of Fabiola going to Hollywood with Brad, and she was engulfed in a sea of sharp jealousy. Lucky girl, she thought bitterly. She's getting away from this place and all its troubles.

Later that afternoon Vonnie stuck her head in the door of the shop as she was leaving for Santa Fe. "I'm going to have a live model on Monday for you all to work on. That should be a challenge."

"A live model! Who?"

"Miss New Mexico, no less."

"Do you mean Fabiola Manteau?"

"I believe that's the name. All I know is that she is a lovely girl who should make a good model. I also have her lined up to pose for a couple of my classes in Santa Fe."

"Well, have a good weekend."

"You, too."

"I will. My Shoney is coming to Santa Fe to visit me."

"Your Shoney?"

"Oui, my Shoney." With a toss of her long dark hair and a musical laugh, Vonnie was gone.

Grace turned back to her work, thinking how Vonnie had come a long way to find her dream man, and Shoney had waited a long time for his dream girl. "They really are perfect for each other," she said outloud.

The rest of the day was uneventful until an eastern tourist stopped by and ordered an expensive Indian blanket in turquoise and white, specifying that it must have a horse pattern woven into it. "White horses running around in a circle," she said. Grace told her she would order the blanket from one of her weavers in Chimayo and send it to her within three months.

A short time later as Grace was getting ready to close, Jimmy came striding in. "Sorry I haven't seen much of you lately," he said hastily.

Grace folded her arms over her chest. "Well, do you want to tell me why I haven't seen you? Are you spending all your time marching with the strikers?"

Jimmy looked down at the floor and then slowly lifted his head and gazed straight at his questioner. "Actually, I helped with a fire yesterday."

"Where?" Grace asked cooly.

"At Adele and Eric's house. Shoney and I had a tip that the Anderson house was pinpointed to be burned because Eric and his brothers are still working, so we hid in the house and waited. About dusk we heard some thuds on the roof, and we crept out the back door and climbed the hill behind their house and caught the culprits throwing firebrands on the roof. It was Bill McKane and some striking miners. We chased them down the hill and beat the living hell out of them. Shoney gave McKane a chance to make good on the threats he's been making, and the bully came out on the short end of the stick. The Anderson boys and I took care of the rest of them. The last we saw they were running to get in their car parked at the foot of the hill. I don't think they'll be back there anymore."

"Where was Adele?" Grace asked in a stunned voice.

"In the house, and when we went after the strikers, she calmly climbed up on the roof and threw the firebrands off. She's a trooper, that Adele. They didn't cause any damage to the house."

Grace shuddered. "I hate this strike," she said accusingly.

Jimmy gently placed his hands on her shoulders. "I hate it, too. Don't you ever believe I don't." He looked deeply into her angry eyes, quietly willing her to keep faith in him.

Grace pulled back and lashed out. "Well, you're not working. You're apparently on the side of the strikers."

"I've told you they have some valid points. But I also told you I don't believe in violence." Jimmy put his arms around Grace and tried to pull her to him in spite of her resistance.

"Just be patient, Tex. This will all be over before long, and then we can be together again."

Pushing him away, the irate girl stood up straight. "You take too much for granted, Jimmy Kirkwood. I don't have to sit here and wait for you or anybody else." Stepping back out of arm's reach, she added, "Go on and do your strike business. I wouldn't want to interfere with whatever you're doing."

"As a matter of fact, Grace, I do have a meeting to go to tonight—a very important meeting. Remember when you told me not too long ago that I would make a good negotiator?" Jimmy searched her eyes for understanding.

"I suppose I do," Grace said icily.

"Well, that's what I'm trying to be. I'm hoping to get some compromise on both sides so we can get this thing settled. As I said, Grace, have some faith in me, please."

Grace stood as stiff as an ice queen. "Maybe I'm tired of having faith in you. Maybe my dad has been right about you all along. Maybe I can do more important things than wait for you to get your strike business done."

Jimmy's face twisted in pain as if he had been physically struck. "You don't mean what you're saying, Grace."

"I am saying," Grace retorted, her whole body emanating anger, "I will not be treated this way, Jimmy! I refuse to be ignored and forgotten as you pursue whatever it is you are pursuing, because, Mr. Striker, there are plenty other fish in the pond."

Jimmy's body visibly sagged into agonizing defeat. "I've got to go, Grace. We'll talk about this later." He sighed and turned to leave.

18

The day was cold and crisp as Grace and Brad headed up the Pecos Road to Tererro. Halfway up Elk Mountain they took a cut-off that led to Rico and Gifford Towns. "I'll show you two of the villages that are part of Tererro," Grace said.

Brad looked over at his riding partner and smiled. She wore jodhpurs and riding boots topped by a heavy wool jacket and mittens. A green wool scarf around her neck partially covered her face. The only clues to the perfect features which had attracted his attention were her extraordinary gray eyes, shining now with excitement. He had come to lure another girl to Hollywood, but he found himself much more interested in this naive Texas beauty. She had the innocent appeal of a young deer frolicking in the woods. She was completely unaware of the assault on his mind and senses which occurred as she smiled and talked of the mountain country she loved so much.

"This is Rico Town," she announced as they arrived at a small village. Curious children with big dark eyes ran out to gaze at the twosome when they passed. Lumber houses built in no special plan huddled together as if for security. "The Spanish and Mexican workers live here," Grace explained.

"The company must provide the lumber for these houses," Brad said. "Usually you see adobe houses where Mexican and Spanish people live."

They continued up the steep road until they finally came to another group of lumber houses. "This is Gifford Town," Grace said. "Mostly Anglo people live here. The company sawmill is located just up Indian Creek. It provides all the lumber for the mining operations as well as for any houses the workers want to build," Grace went on to explain. Her thoughts shifted suddenly to the little log cabin with the lumber addition Jimmy was adding, and quick tears burned her eyes. "Let's drop by my friend's house," Grace said hastily as she quickly brushed a mittened hand across her face.

They stopped in front of a house that was somewhat larger than the other dwellings. It had more than the usual two rooms, and its exterior was attractively covered with pine slabs. A small garage was set to the side in the trees.

"Looks like Adele has the fanciest home in Gifford Town," Grace said with satisfaction. "Let's see if she's home." They tied their horses to a pine tree by the garage and stepped up to the porch.

Grace knocked loudly on the heavy wooden door, but there was no response. She was about to give up when the door opened and Adele peeked out. After a moment's hesitation she stood in the open doorway smiling.

"Whut in the world are you doin' here?" she asked, genuinely surprised.

"Adele, you remember Bradley Thornton?"

"Shore," Adele said, smiling. "Come on in."

A wonderful smell wafted from Adele's kitchen as they passed through the living room, which was furnished with a few wooden chairs and a rocking chair and a comfortable looking feather bed on the far end.

A large table with a red checkered cloth dominated the middle of the kitchen. "Sit down," Adele said, "and I'll git you some coffee and a cinnamon roll. I jest finished some prune whip, too. I'll give you a sample o' that little treat. You must be cold and hungry after yore ride up the hill. Here, take off yore coats and be comfortable."

"Brad, you are about to taste some of the best food in the West," Grace said as they sat down.

Adele wore a simple house dress which was clean and starched and ironed to perfection. Her red hair was pulled back in a loose bun, and her plain face was glowing. "You look very happy, Adele," Grace said.

Adele nodded, her face reddening. "I jest took these rolls out o' the oven," she said, smiling as she set her plump golden brown rolls before her guests. "I think I got a pretty good 'do' on my bread dough today, so they should be fit'n to eat."

"You actually made these rolls yourself?" Brad asked in amazement as he took a bite.

"O' course," Adele replied, another smile coming to her face. "They's nobody else around here to cook 'em."

"They're wonderful," Brad continued. "I've never eaten anything in Hollywood so good."

"Maybe that's a good reason for you to move to the Pecos. Dad could probably get you a job in the mine," Grace teased as she looked at the city man with amusement.

"They ain't hirin' now," Adele said quickly. "You know, with the strike and all."

"I know," Grace said with a giggle. "I'm just giving this Hollywood fellow a bad time."

"You haven't had any more fire scares, have you?" Grace asked, the mention of the strike injecting a more serious tone to the conversation.

"Nope," Adele responded. "And I've got a loaded gun if'n anybody th'ows another fireband on my roof, and don't think I won't use it."

Grace knew she would. "Hopefully it won't happen again. The men who did it should have learned a lesson after what happened to them." She and Adele exchanged knowing looks.

Adele went over to a counter and started ladling a rich brown mixture into thick china bowls. "I'll give you a taste o' my prune whip dessert I'm makin' for the men tonight," Adele said as she set the bowls in front of her guests.

"How many men do you have?" Brad asked.

"Three," Adele answered. "My husband and his two brothers. But I got plenty o' prune whip. I made a big batch."

Grace took a small bite and felt the sweet creamy delight melt in her mouth. "It's scrumptious!" Grace said. "How do you make it?"

"I save the cream from the top o' the milk we git from the dairy, and when thar's enough, I mix it with cooked prunes and sugar and a little cinnamon and whip it all together. I made up the recipe myself, and the men like it," Adele explained. "'Sides, it's good fer digestion."

When they had finished, Brad leaned back with a satisfied sigh. "We aren't going to have any room for our Tererro dinner tonight."

"You shouldn't be going over there, anyways," Adele said, frowning. "Trouble is breakin' out there all the time, 'specially when the workers go through the strike lines."

"Well, we aren't going to go hungry after this feast anyway," Grace said. "We'll just ride up to the baseball field and over to the golf course."

"Suits me fine," Brad said as he got up from the table. "We'd better be on our way, don't you think, Grace?"

"Yes, we've got some more country to cover," she replied, putting on her coat, scarf, and mittens, and giving Adele a hug. "Thanks so much for the delicious food. Eric is a very lucky man to have you for a wife."

"I'm the lucky one," Adele said quietly. "He's a good man."

"What an amazing woman," Brad said as they headed out into the cold mountain air.

"And a good friend," Grace added.

As the riders passed Dora Ortiz's house, they noticed a little red haired girl playing outside. "Hello, Carmen," Grace said, waving. "How is Dora doing?"

"She's married and working in Albuquerque," the little girl shyly replied. "And Ramon is in the Army now."

"Tell Dora I said hello," Grace said.

The young girl smiled and turned to go in the house. I'd like to capture that special sweetness in her face, Grace thought. Next spring I'll come up here and sketch her among the wild flowers.

Brad and Grace were soon riding around the bases at the baseball diamond, and Grace was telling Brad about the team's winning last year's championship. She suddenly pictured the fiesta celebration in Santa Fe when Jimmy later asked her to marry him. It seemed so long ago, she thought sadly. Her eyes misted as she quickly turned. "Let's head for the golf course now."

"I can't believe that miners have a golf course," Brad said.

"Well, they don't play on it much. Mostly the bosses use it."

"I should have brought my clubs," Brad said, "but I had no idea this facility would be here."

Soon they were down the mountain to a large meadow where the golf course lay, everything very professionally manicured. "Someone knew what he was doing when he planned this course," Brad said, looking around approvingly.

"My dad plays here," Grace said. "And really enjoys it."

"Let's sit over on this green in the sun for a few minutes," Brad said as he stepped off his horse.

"You know, you ride pretty well," Grace said. "I wasn't sure you would be such a good horseman, coming from the city."

"I haven't always lived in the city," Brad said, as he took her arm. "I'm really a country boy at heart. I was born in Ohio."

"Really?" Grace said in surprise. "I would never have thought that."

"Well, I've been in California quite a while. I went to Hollywood to become a big star. I didn't make it but now have a good job with a motion picture company."

"That sounds exciting," Grace said, looking up into Brad's clear blue eyes.

"It's exciting when I meet people like you," Brad said as he took her hand.

Grace lowered her eyes, feeling a little breathless and a little confused all at once. She studied a small pyrite pebble in the sand in a quick effort to hide her flustered face.

"I want to talk to you seriously for a minute," Brad said as Grace slowly raised her eyes to meet his. "I'll be taking Fabiola back to Hollywood with me, as you know. Her mother is coming also. They'll try it for a while and see what happens."

"How nice," Grace said, sincerely happy for the girl.

"But, I have talked to my boss about you, too, Grace. I've told him I have discovered another girl in Tererro who I think will make a star. I'm talking about you, Grace."

Brad paused to let his words sink into the startled girl. "Do you understand, Grace? I'm talking about you."

"You can't mean me," Grace said, not believing what she had just heard.

"I do mean you," Brad said. "You're a beautiful girl, Grace. Don't you realize that?"

"I guess I look all right," Grace said slowly. "but I never thought of being beautiful. My mother was beautiful, but I don't look anything like her. I look like my father's family. I look like my Aunt Rosa." Grace suddenly closed her mouth and shook her head in confusion.

"Oh yes, you are beautiful, Grace. You look like a pretty Katherine Hepburn. Have you ever seen her picture?"

Grace thought of her movie star scrap book and nodded her head.

"Well, that's the way you look, only better. You're a classy natural beauty, Grace. Take my word for it. You are just that."

Grace drew her hand away as the possibility of exciting new horizons unfolded before her. "What are you trying to say, exactly, Brad?"

"I would like to take you back to Hollywood with me, too," Brad replied getting up. "How does that appeal to you?"

The overwhelmed girl suddenly lowered her head and put her slim artistic hands over her eyes as if to bring herself back to reality. "I can't think, Brad. I'm sorry, but I just can't think. Maybe we'd better start back."

"May I come with you and talk to your father?" Brad persisted.

"I guess so," Grace said softly.

"Well, come on, let's go," Brad said. "This may be the beginning of a new life for you, Grace."

As Grace rode quietly beside the man who was promising her a dream almost beyond comprehension, she felt contradictory waves of elation and terror flooding her body. What am I going to do? she kept asking herself over and over. And what about Jimmy?

Brad silently let the young girl digest his offer. He wouldn't push her, but he knew she was interested, and he hoped to persuade her father to let her go with him. He believed this beautiful girl had a chance at stardom, and more than that, he was beginning to realize he truly wanted to keep her in his life.

Twenty minutes later they were home, and the Studebaker was not in the yard. "Dad's not here," Grace said.

"I'll go on to the lodge," Brad said. "You think about what I've said, and I'll try to see both of you tomorrow."

Just as Brad turned his horse to leave, a car came up the driveway. "Oh, it's Jimmy," Grace said in surprise.

"Who's Jimmy?" Brad asked, reining in his horse.

Grace didn't have time to answer before Jimmy jumped out of the car and stomped over to the two riders. "Been out to see the country?" he asked brusquely, looking directly at Brad.

"Yes," Brad said with a smile. "Grace has been showing me some of the sights around Tererro. We had a good ride, but I'm just leaving. I'll see you later, Grace." Brad dug his heels into his horse's sides and left at a fast lope.

"What are you doing with him?" Jimmy demanded. "You've got no business with that city slicker."

"I may have a lot of business with him for all you know," Grace said defensively, looking down from her horse into Jimmy's irate face.

"You have no business with him," Jimmy repeated angrily.

Grace's face flushed, and she lashed out, "Don't tell me what to do, Jimmy Kirkwood. You haven't been interested enough in me lately to even come and see me, so what right have you got to care who I am with, or what I am doing?"

"You've forgotten one very important thing, Grace. I asked you to marry me, and you said you would," Jimmy said quietly. "Or have you forgotten?"

Grace held up her left hand. "Do you see a ring here?"

"No...but..."

"No, you're right. So, therefore, I am not promised to you or to anyone. I will do what I want to do, and I do not have to answer to you for any reason. You might as well get that straight right now."

Jimmy looked at Grace a moment longer as the blood drained from his face. "It's straight," he said through clenched teeth, and then jumped into his car and spun out of the yard.

19

As Jimmy spun down the road, Grace turned Duchess around and headed for the Owens' house. Maybe a short visit with my friends will make me feel better, she said to herself.

The Owens family had just finished supper when Grace arrived. "Let me help you with the dishes," she said, grateful for the distraction.

Grace quickly dried the dishes and then washed up the milk separator parts. Mrs. Owens fed the animals while Mike and Tommy hung around the kitchen watching Grace sponge off the counters and the table and the stove. She loved the big wood range with blue porcelain oven doors. It might be fun to cook on a stove like this, she thought wistfully.

"You're pretty good help in the kitchen," Tommy said, breaking the silence.

Grace looked over at him with a smile as her depressed thoughts faded somewhat. Thinking of a book she had recently read about palm reading, she took Tommy's hand in hers. "You're so right, Tommy. Let me show you what else I can do—I can tell your fortune."

Grace's audience was under her spell as they stared at the hand she was intently studying. I've got them in my power, she realized. Now to make up some good stories . . .

"All right, Mike," she began in a low dramatic voice. "I see a long lifeline here in the middle of your hand. I see a happy childhood, and then a sickness tries to invade your body when you are about twenty-five. But by that time you are married to a pretty blonde girl, and she takes care of you, and you get well." Tommy hooted at the mention of a blonde girl in Mike's future.

"You will have a long married life, and let's see how many children you and your wife will have." Grace turned Mike's hand over and studied the side of it below his little finger. "Oh, I see four children, all girls. See these little lines here. They are your children." Grace pointed to some dim marks on the side of his hand.

"No way," he said firmly, jerking his hand away. "I ain't goin' to have girls."

As Tommy continued laughing at Mike, Grace turned her attention to him. "Well, let's see how many children you will have."

Tommy clasped his hands behind him and turned in circles as Grace tried to grab a hand. "I don't want my fortune told," he protested.

Just then Cora Owens came into the kitchen. "What are you boys doing?" she asked sharply.

"It isn't us," Tommy blurted out. "She wants to tell my fortune."

Mrs. Owens smiled. "Let's leave it to the gypsies, Grace. They'll be here in the spring and we'll turn Tommy over to them."

"No, you won't," Tommy said, looking alarmed. The boys then scrambled out of the kitchen, leaving Grace and their mother smiling after them. "That's one way to get rid of them," Mrs. Owens said.

The boys had taken Grace's mind off her dilemma, but suddenly the events of the day came back into focus, and she heaved a big sigh and sat down at the kitchen table. "Do you have time to talk to me, Mrs. Owens?"

"Of course, dear," the motherly voice replied. "What's on your mind?" She put a glass of milk and some ginger cookies down in front of Grace. "Have a cookie and tell me your story."

"Well," Grace said hesitantly while nibbling a ginger snap, "this is a complicated story."

"That doesn't surprise me," Mrs. Owens said, nodding. "Is it something about Jimmy? I've heard that you two are seeing each other."

"Yes," Grace said, sighing again. "And we're not getting along very well. I seldom see him anymore, and he is critical of everything I do."

"Like what?"

"Like not wanting me to have anything to do with anyone but him. I think he's possesive of me."

"He probably is. Most men are. They like to keep their women for their own private property," Mrs. Owens said matter-of-factly.

"And he's too bossy. I know I'm a little spoiled, but I don't like him telling me what to do," Grace continued.

"That's what all men do," Mrs. Owens said with a chuckle. "But we figure out ways to do just about as we please in spite of them. Don't worry too much about his bossiness."

Talking to Mrs. Owens made Grace feel better. Afterall, here was a woman who had been married for a long time, and if she didn't feel upset about what Grace was telling her, maybe it wasn't that serious. But there was still Bradley Thornton and Hollywood. She knew she needed to discuss that situation.

Grace swallowed hard and continued. "Mrs. Owens, I've made a friendship with a man from Hollywood. You know, the one who is here to sign up Fabiola Manteau."

The older woman looked at Grace with sharp eyes. "I've heard about him. I hope you aren't letting this relationship go beyond friendship."

"Oh no!" Grace quickly assured her. "But he's telling me that I may also have motion picture star potential. Do you think I should take him seriously?"

Mrs. Owens clasped her hands in front of her chin, digesting the situation for a long minute. "I would think very carefully about this, Grace. Of course, he must talk with your father."

"He was going to, but Dad wasn't home. He's never home anymore. That's something else that's bothering me, Mrs. Owens."

Cora Owens gently patted Grace on the hand. "It's a stressful time for company men," she said quietly. "And your father may also have some personal decisions to make now. Be patient with him, Grace."

"He's not very patient with me," Grace said, frowning.

Mrs. Owens looked thoughtful for a few moments. Finally she said, "Grace, life is very complicated for you right now. I don't have any magic solutions, but I will say this, and I'm sure I'm right. Don't worry too much about Jimmy and your father. If they can't pay you the attention you want right now, there must be good reasons for their actions. In the long run I think you will understand. Don't be too hasty in your judgments."

"I hope you're right," Grace said uncertainly.

"As far as the Hollywood scout goes, be careful in making a decision, and don't do anything until you talk with your father. I can see why you have caught this man's eye. You are truly a very lovely girl, but there are many things to consider."

"I know I've probably handled everything all wrong," Grace said with a break in her voice.

Mrs. Owens put her arm around Grace. "On the contrary, I think you've probably handled things fairly well. Now, I want you to quit worrying so much. Take your time, be patient, and things will work out. I promise you. I've been around quite a long time, and I know what I'm talking about."

Grace looked up into the woman's concerned eyes. "I do feel better, Mrs. Owens. Thank you so much for listening."

Mrs. Owens gave Grace a warm embrace. "You'll do fine. Don't underestimate yourself. And now you'd better get home while there's still light."

Grace went to bed as soon as she got home and tried to go to sleep, but too many restless thoughts kept jumping around in her head. Finally she heard her father come in the front door. Now maybe I can go to sleep, she told herself. She sighed and turned over just as her father opened her bedroom door a crack.

"Are you asleep, Grace?" he asked quietly.

"I'm awake," Grace replied, sitting up in bed.

"Come in and talk with me a few minutes," he said.

Grace felt a moment of panic as she pulled on her robe and hurried into the kitchen. Had her father found out about her engagement to Jimmy or her relationship with Brad? "What's the matter, Dad," she guardedly asked.

"Leota wants you to take over the art class in the morning."

"What's wrong with Vonnie? Is she sick?" she asked, concern replacing panic.

"No, but I'm sure she feels very bad." The strange tone in her father's voice caused her to shiver as feelings of dread permeated her body.

"What are you trying to tell me, Dad?" she asked anxiously.

"Sit down, dear, and I'll get us both some milk." John went to the icebox, opening the door very deliberately. He took out a bottle of milk and carefully set it on the table. Then he placed two glasses on the table with the same deliberate movements. Grace wanted to scream at him as he slowly poured the milk.

"Be patient," Mrs. Owens had said. But Grace knew she wasn't a very patient person.

John took a long drink of milk, closed his eyes, and then opened them as tears rolled down his face. "Shoney was found in his car tonight with a bullet hole in his head. He was coming home from Santa Fe. He had spent the weekend there with Vonnie."

A picture of Vonnie's face flashed in Grace's mind as she remembered seeing her on Friday when she stopped by the gift shop. Now she knew the glow on her face had been because Shoney would be visiting.

"Oh, no," Grace said weakly, putting her head down on the table and realizing how trivial her problems were in comparison to Vonnie's tragedy. Lifting her eyes, she looked into her father's stricken face. "What happened?"

"All we know is that he was shot in about the same place along the road where Mr. Dodson was murdered. Jimmy found him when he was on patrol. He went to the lodge and called the Pecos deputy. Then he went to Santa Fe to tell Vonnie. She asked if you could take her classes this next week."

"How did you find out about all this?" Grace asked.

"I was at the lodge when Jimmy came to call the deputy."

You were with Leota, Grace thought. But strangely, she felt no bitterness. She knew it was time to accept the idea of Leota and her father. Obviously there was no longer any choice in the matter.

Grace suddenly felt as if she were the stronger of the two. Coming around the table to her father, she hugged his bent shoulders. "We must get some rest now, Dad. We'll think about this tomorrow."

Grace gave her father a kiss as he headed for his bedroom. "Try to get some sleep," she said. "We both have to work tomorrow. In fact, I have to be a teacher. Dad, did you ever think this girl of yours who didn't start school until she was eight years old would ever be a teacher?"

John smiled weakly at his daughter and went to his bedroom.

Later, Grace lay like a frozen statue in her bed. Big strong Shoney Terrell dead? How could that be true? And what was Jimmy doing patrolling the Pecos Road? That's what Dad said he was doing. He was patrolling the road when he found Shoney.

Is that why I haven't seen much of him lately? Because he's patrolling? Why is he patrolling?

Her mind was dizzy with the thoughts that whirled through her head. Well, he isn't working, yet he's the one who discovered Bill McKane trying to burn down Adele's house. Was he patrolling that night, too?

The exhausted girl turned over with a sigh. Tears of sadness filled her eyes, but her thoughts were for others this time. Poor, poor Shoney. And poor, dear Vonnie.

20

Grace took over her responsibilities in the art class with resolve. "I hope to make Miss Messier proud of us while she's away," she told the class. "Her teaching is an inspiration, and when she comes back next week, I want her to be able to see in our strokes the love and compassion we are feeling for her. Remember, she has told us that many artists accomplish their best work after heartrending emotional crises."

Grace looked around at the intent faces of the students. "This week we are shadowed by sorrow because of what has happened in the life of our beloved teacher. We will put our emotions on canvas as a tribute to Miss Messier and the love of her life, Shoney Terrell."

At that moment, a beautiful young woman appeared in the doorway, holding out her hand to Grace as a compassionate smile complemented her perfect facial features. "I'm Fabiola," she said in a low husky voice. "Do you remember me?"

"Of course, Fabiola. I'm so sorry. I'm not quite myself this morning," Grace said, going to welcome her.

"I know," Fabiola said as she squeezed Grace's hand warmly. "I heard and understand perfectly. Forgive me, but I listened to your opening words to the class. I am impressed but would never have thought you would gravitate to the teaching field."

"I'm more surprised than anyone," Grace said. "This is only temporary, of course, but I think I'm going to enjoy it."

"You will do very well," Fabiola said as she patted Grace's shoulder with a well manicured hand. "But, I hope you won't be disappointed today. I'm not going to be able to pose for your class since it will be necessary to leave sooner than I had thought when I made the arrangements with Miss Messier. I do apologize."

"I think just meeting Miss New Mexico will suffice for our class," Grace said graciously. "Students, I want you all to meet Miss Fabiola Manteau who recently won the crown of Miss New Mexico. She's from Tererro, and I went to school with her. I'm not surprised she has won this honor. She was always a very outstanding girl."

"It is my pleasure to meet all of you," Fabiola said, favoring the art students with a stunning smile. "But I really must go." Turning to Grace she said, "Good luck with your teaching."

"Good luck to you," Grace said sincerely, as the class clapped appreciatively, and Fabiola walked gracefully out the classroom door.

"Let's get to work, everybody," Grace said, turning to her easel.

Grace was painting a young girl kneeling in prayer beside a worn rocking chair. She had been thinking of her mother when she started the painting. Now her thoughts turned to Vonnie, and the depiction began to resemble her as Grace swirled in the long dark curls falling back in chaos from the suffering face. Tears glistened on dark lashes, and her lips seemed to tremble. I hadn't been able to get the right expression on her face before now, Grace thought.

The new teacher spent part of the morning visiting with each student about his or her work. She found satisfaction in helping the young artists achieve the moods and effects they were striving for as they made subtle additions and changes to their canvases under her direction.

When the class was over, Grace felt a deeper satisfying sense of accomplishment than she had ever experienced before. She then went around the room and glanced with approval at the artwork. "The day went fine," she told herself.

Grace was just about to leave when Leota walked in. "How did it go?" she asked.

"All right, I think. We had a good class in spite of our depressed feelings."

"I knew you could do it," Leota said as she noted how tired Grace looked. She turned to go but then hesitated. "Why don't you take the rest of the week off from the gift shop. There won't be many customers because of the strike and the trouble we have here. If anyone wants something, I'll open up for them."

"That would help," Grace said. "I want to go to Shoney's funeral, and then I'd also like to go to see Vonnie. Thanks so much. But if you need help, let me know."

"You just keep the art class going, and don't worry about the gift shop," Leota said as she scurried out of the room with her usual quick steps.

As Grace came out the front door of the lodge and started toward her car, someone called her name. For a moment it didn't register that the man approaching was Bradley Thornton. She hadn't thought of him or their ride together since the chaotic events of last night.

As Brad hurried up to her in all his energetic good looks, Grace felt her heart immediately skip a beat. "I need to talk to you," he said breathlessly. "I want to discuss my proposal with you and your father."

"Your proposal?" Grace asked blankly.

"Don't tell me you've forgotten about my offer to take you to Hollywood," Brad said, looking exasperated.

"Oh that," she said quickly. "I guess I did forget. I'm really sorry, Brad."

"Do you want me to give you more time to think about this?" Brad asked, sensing her preoccupation. "I had planned to leave tomorrow, but I could change my plans."

Grace's heart had stopped thumping, and she looked at Brad with level and determined eyes. At that moment she felt no more confusion.

"I'm not going to Hollywood with you, Brad," she said, knowing in her heart this was the right decision. "I've got other things I have to do here, very important things. Now I'm tired, and I'm going home."

"Going to Hollywood isn't one of the things you'll be considering?" Brad asked quietly.

"No," Grace said brightly. "But I wish you and Fabiola all the luck in the world there." With a smile and a wave, she stepped quickly into her car.

"Damn!" Brad said, standing in the Studebaker's dust. "She could have made both of us famous." He scowled after the departing car for a few moments, and then turned back toward his cabin. "Oh well, there are lots of other pretty girls. Might as well get out of this place tomorrow."

Grace sped down the Pecos Road with a heart that felt lighter than it had for several days. There's one problem solved, she told herself with a sense of relief. Maybe it will all work out, as Mrs. Owens said.

The day was heavily overcast, but the temperature was mild as Grace spotted Duchess standing in the pasture. She headed up the driveway and spontaneously decided to go for a ride. "Give me a few minutes to get changed, Dutch Girl, and we'll have a little outing. Maybe the fresh air will help clear my head."

Duchess pranced up the deserted Pecos Road as her mistress breathed in the crisp air and felt her stressed senses revive. "Let's go up Willow Creek," Grace said to her faithful friend. "We'll stop and visit Mrs. Owens on our way back."

Suddenly, without any warning, a car careened around them, flinging gravel into the air. "What the heck?" Grace said, putting an arm up to shield her face.

As the dust settled, Grace noticed that the speeding vehicle was bigger and fancier than those driven by anyone in Tererro or Pecos.

The car then turned swiftly onto the Willow Creek cut-off. "Why would they be going up there?" Grace wondered aloud.

"Well, let's just see what's going on," she muttered to her little mare.

As Grace and Duchess reached the place where the car had turned off, she glanced up the hill and spotted two men climbing up the mountain, headed in the direction of Indian Cave. She quietly pulled Duchess over into a thick pine grove and watched the men through the branches until they reached the cave entrance and vanished inside.

Grace then moved cautiously closer. "I don't know why I'm doing this, Dutch," she whispered.

The perplexed girl sat transfixed in her secluded spot for a long time and was just getting ready to start for home when the two men came out of the cave, each carrying a small rectangular box. Their load seemed to be heavy, and the men walked slowly and carefully down the mountain to the car. They put their boxes in the trunk and then leaned against the side of a tree.

One of them looks like Bill McKane, Grace told herself nervously. And what are they hanging around for, I wonder.

Finally the men started back up to the cave and dropped out of sight in a clump of trees. As Grace watched, only one of them reappeared, so she continued to watch intently through the trees for the other man.

Suddenly Duchess perked up her ears and gave a nervous whinny. "Easy," Grace said hastily as she tightened the reins. Just as she reached down to pat her horse's neck, she felt herself being propelled through the air and then falling with a thud to the ground. Darkness engulfed her as she vainly struggled to fight her way back to light and life.

21

Grace fought to regain her awareness in the total darkness of a strange and frightening new world. Her eyelids fluttered, and slowly she realized she was lying on her side with one arm thrown over her face. She didn't move as she tried to understand what had happened.

She could see a beam of light flashing in the darkness, and the sound of voices suddenly broke the silence, penetrating her confusing environment. Grace closed her eyes and lay still, hardly breathing. She felt her arm being raised briefly and then released to fall back over her face. "She's still out," an unfamiliar voice said. "We'll leave her here. She ain't goin' nowhere."

The voice moved away, and the mumbling conversation was too soft for her to make out. She cracked her eyes and again saw beams of light criss-crossing around her. Desperately trying to regain consciousness, Grace finally began to process her new surroundings. *Where am I? What has happened to me?*

The voices became clearer as the men moved closer. "We gotta get this stuff loaded up so we can take care of our project tonight," Grace heard. "We'll come back and tend to her later. If she wakes up she can't go no place, and if she does try to get out o' here, the chances are she'll get lost inside the cave. And, we'll just let her stay there if that happens. Come on, we gotta make tracks. We're late already."

I'm in Indian Cave! Grace suddenly realized. She cracked her eyelids open slightly as the men walked away and then frantically searched her surroundings while the light briefly flashed around her. Quickly she scanned the wall in the dim light. We left a candle up there, she remembered. Yes! To the right on the little ledge. Blackness overtook her again, and she closed her eyes while her thoughts swirled dizzily. Oh, my head hurts, she thought, and she fought the weakness which was trying to overcome her body.

The light faded, and Grace lay still for several minutes before she had the strength to sit up. I've got to get out of here, she told herself with quiet resolve. I'm sure one of those men was Bill McKane, and he's definitely up to no good.

Finally she lifted her trembling body and rested on her knees. She waited a few more minutes before pulling herself upright as she clawed the hard wall, clinging to the rocks for support. But her fickle legs turned to water, and she crumpled to the cave floor. She rested until feeling her strength return, and again pulled her faltering body to a standing position while stretching her hand gingerly up the rock wall to find the candle. "You can't fool me," she said aloud to the darkness. "I know it's there."

But her groping fingers felt no rock ledge or candle. She was getting weaker and knew she would pass out again if she didn't sit down. She eased herself back to the floor of the cave and gratefully rested a few minutes as the swirling darkness in her head rivaled the darkness in the cave.

I've got to get the candle, Grace thought desperately. She tried again and again, but each time sank back to the floor in weak despair.

After another lengthy rest, Grace finally felt her strength once more begin to renew, and her head started to clear. "Okay. I must stand up and move two steps to the right. If I don't feel the candle, I'll move back two steps to the left," she planned out loud.

Her reasoning worked. As she moved to the right and reached high, her fingers closed on the rock shelf. Carefully, she brought the candle and some matches down and held them to her breast with both hands. "I did it, I did it!" she said, tears running down her cheeks.

Grace was trembling too much to light the candle, so she sat down again and waited to gain control of her emotions and her body.

Then the words of the men came back to her. "We'll take care of her later." Her mind suddenly felt alert and coldly calculating. She knew she had to work fast and get out of the cave. She had to warn someone so Bill McKane's evil plans could be thwarted.

Holding the candle in her left hand, Grace raked the match across the rock wall, and mercifully, it flared into a flickering light. Her heart beat faster as she held the wick to the flame. Then she opened her eyes wide to adjust to the light as she clutched the candle with both hands. But Grace suddenly realized she couldn't leave yet. "I must see what they have back here," she murmured as she moved farther into the cave, in spite of her body's strong desire to go the other direction.

Grace made out some wooden boxes stacked by the side of the wall. She held the candle down to reveal the word, EXPLOSIVES, printed on the boxes.

"Oh dear God," she groaned. "Those men are going to blow something up."

Turning quickly, Grace started for the entrance of the cave with new resolve. Thank God I know the way out, she thought.

The unsteady girl hurried down the passageway, feeling the same panicky emotions she had experienced in the cave before. Finally she was out in the bright daylight, leaving the ominous darkness behind her.

As Grace stumbled awkwardly down the hill from the cave, she looked around for Duchess. Not seeing her, she tried to plan what her next move would be. I'll walk to the Owens' house, she decided. Yes, Mrs. Owens will know what to do.

But she immediately changed her strategy and headed for the dairy barns. Maybe Mr. Owens will be there tending to the cows, she hoped.

As Grace neared the barns, she spotted Duchess standing by the corrals. Poor girl, Grace thought. She's confused and lost.

"Come on, Dutch. Come on, girl," Grace said softly.

Duchess whirled and trotted over to the tired girl who was leaning on a boulder to get her breath. Grace then took the reins and patted her neck reassuringly. "We got into a little trouble, didn't we? But it's all right. We're going to be fine now."

Grace struggled to pull herself into the saddle. "I'm sorry, girl," she said as she gasped for air and slid back to the ground. "Just be patient with me."

The weary girl finally mounted and turned her mare toward the house. Tying Duchess to a rail took all her strength, and she slumped down on the porch. "Mrs. Owens, come quickly, please," she called in an exhausted voice.

The door flung open, and Mrs. Owens rushed out, sensing at once something was wrong. "What is it, child? What has happened? Did your horse throw you?"

Grace looked up with a big smile. "I'm fine...now, but I need help."

Cora Owens put her hand to her mouth. "Hen...ry! Hen...ry!" she yelled in a high pitched voice.

An answering "Ho!" drifted back.

"Come to the house quick," Mrs. Owens called back in the same penetrating voice. "Front yard."

"Lordy, she could be heard from here to Kingdom Come," Grace muttered as her head ached from the shrieking notes coming out of the woman's throat.

Henry Owens appeared almost immediately. "I been workin' on that fence in the back," he explained, coming around the corner of the house. "What is it?" he asked in alarm when he saw Grace hunched on the steps.

Grace quickly blurted out her story as Henry listened wide-eyed. He didn't understand exactly what had happened, but there was no question Grace needed to see her father right away. "Leave your horse here," he said. "Let's go find your dad."

Grace leaned her head against the seat of Henry's milk delivery truck as they sped down the road. "You say these men were carrying boxes of explosives out of the cave?" Henry asked, frowning, his eyes glued to the road.

"Yes, that's what they were doing," Grace replied. "Moving boxes of explosives."

Henry looked speculatively at Grace, and then they turned up the back road that would take them to the mine offices. Some striking miners were standing around with signs, but they made no move to stop the truck.

Grace jumped out of the vehicle with renewed energy when Henry pulled to a stop in front of the building that housed the administrative offices. Her father had seen the truck drive up and was waiting for her at the door. "What is it, Grace?" he called with a frown on his face.

"I have to tell you something very important, Dad," Grace replied quickly.

"Come in and sit down," her father said as he showed her into his office. She dropped into a chair, and he took his seat behind his desk. "Tell me what it is, Baby. What has happened?" Deep lines of anxiety cut into his face.

John listened to Grace's story, frequently interrupting to clarify her broken sentences. When the whole terrifying incident had been poured out, he got up and took his daughter in his arms. "Are you hurt anywhere, Grace?"

"My head doesn't feel so good," she replied.

"Poor baby," John said, tenderly stroking her head.

As her father's hand passed over her temple, Grace let out an involuntary cry. "Ouch! That hurts!"

"I'm sure it does," John said softly. "You've got a bump there as big as an egg." He shook his head and frowned. "Just wait until I get my hands on those cowardly coyotes. They can't treat my daughter this way."

"I'll live, Dad. I guess I'm pretty tough after all." Grace looked up at her father with a hint of her impish smile.

"I'll be back in a few minutes," he said, patting her cheek. "I need to speak with Ted Cooper."

Grace sat alone in the comfortable chair and relaxed for the first time in hours. Dad will handle this, she thought. I don't have to worry anymore.

Ten minutes later John came back with Ted Cooper. "Ted and I have come up with a plan," he said quietly. "And we need someone brave and dependable to make it work. You're going to have to help us, Grace, because all of the available men we can trust are guarding the mine site tonight. Do you feel like having another adventure?"

"Sure Dad," Grace said, smiling gamely.

"Now, you're positive the boxes the men were moving contained explosives?" John asked.

"Yes, it was clearly printed on the sides."

"And you're absolutely positive one of the men was Bill McKane?"

"I was pretty groggy, but I'm sure. He talked about needing the explosives for a project tonight."

"Well, Ted and I think we need to get word to the sheriff. The only problem is our telephone lines are down. We suspect these men had something to do with this dilemma, and we don't want to send any of our men to Pecos by car for fear of an ambush. Besides, we need them here to guard the high risk places like the water tower, the school, the businesses, and the boiler." John paused and took Grace's hands in his own. "We need to send someone over the tram line with a message." He paused again, looking steadily into his daughter's eyes. "Could you do that for us, Grace?"

"You mean, ride one of those ore cars on the tram line to Pecos?" she asked in disbelief.

"That's what I'm saying," John assured her. "We need someone absolutely loyal and trustworthy. You are that person, Grace."

The fear that had dominated Grace's day was suddenly replaced with determination and excitement. Her dream of riding the tram line was about to come true.

"We'll walk over to the control building now and load you into an ore car," John continued. "Are you ready?"

Grace's eyes sparkled as she answered with certainty, "Ready!"

22

Grace went with her father and Ted Cooper into the steel building where the ore was loaded into the buckets to be transported twelve miles down the Pecos Canyon. She looked in awe at the huge machinery that controlled the aerial tramway, not knowing that the enormous iron curved beam structure looming up in front of her guided the track ropes on which the cars rode. She looked at the huge steel cables which pulled the cars on their journey back and forth to the mine, and then she saw the most gigantic wheel she had ever seen.

"What is that monstrosity?" she gasped.

"That's the bull wheel which drives the haul rope that pushes the cars," Ted said. "It can push a girl to Alamitos with no trouble."

"We have cut down on running the tram since the strike," John explained to Grace. "We'll put you in the bucket and then start the big generator that will power the line. It will take you a little over an hour to get to the end of the tram. You should watch carefully as you approach the mill and start yelling before you come to the end of the line. There's a watchman there who will help you get out."

"We'll give you a flag to attract attention," Ted Cooper said. "Wave it and yell just before you get there. You'll be able to see the steel buildings and ore piles in a clearing on the mountain in plenty of time.

"You can give this note to the watchman," John said. "It will explain why we need law enforcement help. Tell him to get in touch with the deputy sheriff." John pushed the envelope deep into Grace's jacket pocket.

"He'll call the sheriff's office in Las Vagas," Ted added. "We need more than the deputy from Pecos and the security people here at the mine."

"Jimmy and the deputy are patrolling the roads and bridges, as well as the school and the businesses, so that's why neither of them can make this trip for us," John said.

There was that phrase again, "Jimmy is patrolling," Grace thought.

"Don't worry," Grace said to the two men. "All I have to do is get in the ore car and ride to the end of the tram. Anybody could do that."

"You are carrying very important information. Make sure you give it to the watchman. He's a man with a big black beard and long black hair," John said. "Stay at the mill with the watchman, and I'll be over to get you tonight. I'll wait until San Miguel County Deputies are patrolling the Pecos Road," John explained.

The two men then picked Grace up and lifted her to the top of the six foot ore car. "Grab that bar the car is attached to," John said. "Now crouch down and hang on to the side while you lower yourself into the bucket."

Grace quickly grasped the bar and sat for a moment on the edge of the bucket. Then she released the bar and jumped.

"Are you all right?" John called out when he heard her land on the metal floor.

"Fine," Grace yelled.

"Here's the flag," Ted said as he tossed it over the side of the ore car.

"I'll be at the mill to get you tonight," her father called.

"Starting the engines," Ted yelled.

Standing in one corner of the car, Grace rested her head against the dented iron walls as the bucket slowly started to move. "I'm on my way!" she shouted, wincing as agonizing pain suddenly slashed through her head.

As the bucket gained momentum, Grace heard a faint, "Good luck."

Grace then unfurled the flag and held it up as it rippled in the breeze. She gazed for a moment at the beautiful flag flying in the cloudy gray sky, but then quickly pulled it back down into the bucket. "Can't tip anyone off," she said out loud.

Through a crack in the corner near the floor, Grace could peer down from her sky highway. She spotted the mine buildings fading away and could make out the winding Pecos River flowing from the town of Tererro to Pecos. The view below looked peaceful and familiar, but the sky above appeared uncertain and threatening. It looks like snow, she thought as she sat down in a corner of the bucket.

The ride was smooth and relaxing, and Grace's weary head soon dropped down on her chest. The sharp pain had settled down to a dull persistent throb. Not a good time for a headache, she thought wryly.

When Grace opened her eyes and quickly looked out, she could still see the Pecos Road, but suddenly her eyes focused on the Ponderosa Lodge below her. "I'm half way there!" she announced to the clouds with satisfaction.

As she sat quietly, her thoughts went back over the day's events. Although it seemed like an eternity ago, it had been only a few hours since she fell into the hands of Bill McKane and his henchman. "You thought you had me, but you didn't," Grace said aloud in a steely voice.

You, Gracie Girl, are always wishing for adventures, she thought as she gingerly felt the contusion on the side of her aching head. I think you got more than you bargained for this time!

Looking out again through the crack a little later, Grace could see nothing but the tops of forested mountains. "I should be getting close to the mill," she reasoned aloud.

Later Grace stood up and put out her mittened hand to catch the soft lacey snowdrops which had started falling from the sky. Winter is here, she thought with satisfaction. Winter with snowmen and sleds and warm fires. Her mind shifted to the little cabin up Indian Creek. She could visualize herself sitting there with Jimmy, drinking hot chocolate and munching on popcorn in front of a blazing fire. But I don't have Jimmy anymore, she sadly reminded herself.

What have we been fighting about? she asked herself. I don't even remember. Well, I know he didn't like me having anything to do with Bradley Thornton.

Grace smiled at the thought of the handsome fellow from Hollywood. He was a pleasant interlude, she admitted. But he's certainly not Jimmy. And no one could tempt me into leaving the mountains and the Pecos, not even to be a movie star. Besides, I'd rather be an artist than an actress. All the answers to my problems seem so clear up here, she marveled.

Suddenly a big snowflake fell on her cheek and melted like a soft kiss. Grace touched her cheek gently. "Mama, did you just put your stamp of approval on my decision? I think you did!"

At that moment, the tops of steel buildings came into view. "The mill!" she gasped, grabbing her flag and waving it energetically. "Hello! Hello! Hello!" she yelled at the top of her voice. "Passenger aboard the ore car!"

The ore car began to slow down. "Hello?" a voice answered.

"You have a person cargo today," Grace said as loudly as she could. "Help me get out." She hardly noticed the sharpened pain in her head as she yelled to the watchman.

The bucket came to a halt with a creaking of cables, and a bushy black head appeared over the top of the rail. "What in tarnation?!"

"I have an important message for you," Grace said, smiling with relief. "Help me get out of this thing."

The bushy head vanished and returned shortly, giving her instructions in a deep voice. "Move to the other end. I've got a ladder so you can climb out."

Grace moved out of the way while the ladder was pushed over the top of the bucket. It clattered to the floor of the car, and Grace quickly leaned it up against the wall. "Coming over," she called out.

The burly man was standing below, reaching his long strong arms up for her. "I'll pull you over. Don't worry, you won't fall. I'll catch you."

Grace closed her eyes in faith as he pulled her out and set her on the ground. "Now tell me, miss, what is this all about?" he demanded.

Grace took the note out of her pocket. "Read this," she said. "It's a matter of life and death, so you must act quickly."

The watchman scanned the letter and started for his office. "Come with me," he called over his shoulder. "I've got to make a call."

The office enveloped Grace with comforting warmth as she walked in the open door. For the first time since starting her trip, she realized how cold she was. Her legs felt wobbly and weak, and her head was pounding as she made her way over to a small cot at the end of the room. I'll just rest a minute, she thought as she eased herself down.

🍎 🍎 🍎

Grace felt as if she had barely closed her eyes when someone gently shook her shoulders. "What do you want?" she mumbled, struggling to open her eyes.

"Wake up, Grace. It's Dad. I'm going to take you home now."

Grace tried to get up, but she was too physically and emotionally exhausted. "I'm sorry, Dad," she said as she felt his strong arms lift her.

"Don't worry, honey," her father said. "I'll take care of you."

23

"Where am I?" Grace asked herself in a small voice as she looked from one white wall to the other.

Her eyes lingered on the window where the sun shone through, casting a warm glow on this strange room. She vaguely remembered snow on her face. It was reassuring just to lie comfortably and enjoy the sunlight. Her body and mind were dormant, and right now she had no desire to bring them to life.

Voices suddenly penetrated her limited world. Two women in white were standing by her bed. "So, you finally woke up. How do you feel."

"I guess I'm fine," Grace answered uncertainly. "Where am I?"

"You're in the Tererro Hospital," said one of the nurses as she stuck a thermometer into her mouth. "Just lie still while we take your temperature and check your blood pressure. I'm Mrs. Smith, and this is Anita," the woman said as she gestured to her helper, an attractive Spanish woman. "You were brought in last night. You have a nasty bump on that pretty head of yours."

Yesterday's events slowly crept back into her consciousness. The men at the cave, the blackness in the cave, the ride on the tram line. Grace quickly closed her eyes to shut out reality, but the ladies in white wouldn't let her escape as they talked and directed, washed and rolled, plumped and pulled, and slipped a clean gown over her head. "Now, you'll feel better," they assured her.

"Anita will bring your breakfast soon. Do you feel hungry?" Mrs. Smith said.

"I don't think so," Grace answered. She didn't really know how she felt. Her head ached, and she just wanted to sleep. She closed her eyes in anticipated rest.

But Anita returned too soon with her breakfast. "I'll raise the head of your bed," she said cheerfully, "and put your food right here in front of you on this little table. You've got coffee, cooked cereal, orange juice, and toast. Doesn't that look good?"

Grace didn't have the energy to explain that she seldom ate any breakfast, and she certainly didn't want to think of eating now. But Anita wasn't leaving, so she took a small drink of the orange juice. It tasted bitter, and she set the glass back on the tray and tried not to make a face.

Anita took two pills from a small cup. "Take these with another sip of orange juice," she directed. Grace reluctantly did as she was told, hoping they would help her headache.

"I'll just put some sugar and milk on your cereal," Anita said helpfully. "That will go down easily and make you feel better."

Grace looked doubtfully at the cereal, but took a small bite under the watchful eyes of her nurse. "Good girl," Anita assured her. "Now, eat all you can. You must get your strength back, you know."

Anita left the room, and Grace toyed with her food for a few minutes longer. She ate a few bites of cereal and toast, but the coffee tasted the best with plenty of sugar and cream. She drank the hot drink slowly while gazing out the window.

Soon, with warm food in her stomach, Grace lay back on her pillow and immediately drifted off to sleep. She was only slightly aware of Anita rolling her bed back down and arranging her covers and pillows.

Hours later, Mrs. Smith gently shook her young patient. "Wake up, Grace. Your father is here to see you."

Grace opened her eyes and tried to raise her head. "I'm sorry," she said as the pain raced through her head again.

"It's all right," came her dad's familiar voice. "Don't try to sit up, Baby. I'll sit with you for a little while."

John took his daughter's hand, and she slowly opened her eyes. "I'm glad you're here, Dad. Am I going to be all right?"

"Of course, darlin'. You got your head bumped, so you need to rest a couple of days. After that, you'll be fine."

Grace smiled and slowly faded back into her dream world.

The next morning when she woke up, Grace felt almost like her old self. She greeted the nurses warmly and sat up on the side of her bed for a while. The pain in her head seemed better.

After breakfast, Grace lay back in bed, reading a magazine Anita had brought her. Dad will be here to see me soon, she told herself as she put her magazine aside. But it was thoughts of Jimmy that dominated her mind. I wonder what he's doing. I don't suppose he'll come to see me. Tears fought at her eyelids as she drifted off to sleep.

Later, the nurses woke Grace for lunch, and she then put on a robe and sat in a wheelchair by the window. The landscape outside was clean and beautiful and white. Snow had covered everything with a fluffy blanket, and the sun was shining brightly on winter's wonderland. Grace could just make out Holy Ghost Creek as it wound its way through the snow mounds. What a picture, she thought. I'll get Dad to bring me some paper so I can sketch it.

Suddenly Grace noticed a law enforcement vehicle plowing through the snow-covered parking lot. I wonder who that is, she thought as she got carefully out of the wheelchair and crawled into bed.

She had just pulled the blankets up when Mrs. Smith opened her door. "Do you feel like talking with someone?" she asked.

"Of course," Grace answered, pleased to think of having company.

The door opened wide and a man in uniform walked slowly into the room. Grace blinked, not believing her eyes. "Jimmy?" she asked in a wavering voice.

"Did you forget me so quickly?" he asked softly as he stood looking down at her, holding his hat over his chest.

"No, of course not," Grace said as Jimmy sat down in a chair by her bed. She looked over at him, and it felt so right to have this special man by her side again.

"I'm so sorry about what you've been through, Tex. It should never have happened. It's my fault."

"I don't see how it could have been your fault," Grace replied. "You weren't even around when I ran into Bill McKane."

Jimmy looked at the pale girl lying in the hospital bed with her head propped up on thick pillows. She appeared so small and fragile, and his heart broke with love and concern for her. "I should have been taking better care of you," he said with a catch in his voice.

Grace was confused by Jimmy's words and also by his looks. "Why are you wearing that uniform?" she asked.

"I'm a deputy sheriff now," Jimmy said. "Actually, I've been with the sheriff's department for quite a while. I've been working undercover since the strike, and I was investigating Bill McKane. The sheriff wanted him watched."

"Is that why you were doing so much patrolling?"

"Yes," Jimmy said with a half-smile.

"Why didn't you tell me?"

"I was sworn to secrecy," Jimmy replied. "It was important that McKane have no idea we were watching him."

"Can you tell me now why you were investigating him?" The sparkle was back in Grace's eyes. This sounded like a real adventure!

"Actually, I can," Jimmy said as he crossed one booted foot over his leg. "Do you remember the sack of tire chains we found in Indian Cave?"

"Yes."

"Well, I told the sheriff about them, and he suspected they might have something to do with the Dodson murder. When the miners struck, I supposedly struck too, but really I was working for the sheriff's office."

"How exciting!" Grace said as her eyes danced. "My Jimmy, an officer!"

Noticing that she referred to him as her personal property brought a smile to Jimmy's serious face. "Then you're not mad at me anymore?"

Grace couldn't remember ever being mad at her hero. Her mama always said she threw a temper tantrum and was over it in five minutes. "Not at all," she said as she looked into his steady brown eyes. No more blue eyes for me, she thought.

Jimmy quickly took her hands. "Honey, do you know what you are saying?"

Grace grinned. "Don't you think I'm in my right mind? I just got a bump on my head. I'm not crazy. Please hold my hands and don't ever let them go." She looked deeply into his dear, familiar eyes. "I'm sorry, Jimmy. I've acted like a child. You're the one who should be angry with me."

"No," Jimmy said. "I should have told you what I was doing, and I should have had that case solved before you got in so much danger. I'll never forgive myself for not taking better care of you. I hope you can forgive me."

"Well then, you're just going to have to take good care of me the rest of your life to make up for that slip of yours. Then maybe I will forgive you."

Jimmy smiled hopefully, but then his face turned questioning. "I heard you were thinking about going to Hollywood with that Bradley fellow."

"Whoever told you that didn't know what they were talking about," Grace responded defensively. "I never told anyone I was going with Brad. I didn't tell him or anyone else."

"He spread the word around, and it was hard to believe you wouldn't," Jimmy said quietly. "It was quite an opportunity."

"Well," Grace said. "I'd much rather live on the Pecos than in Hollywood."

"That's my girl," Jimmy said with happy relief.

"What about Shoney's funeral?" Grace asked, suddenly remembering her friend.

"I just came from there," Jimmy said. "He was buried today in the Veterans Cemetery in Santa Fe."

"That's an appropriate place for Shoney," Grace said as her eyes brimmed with tears. "How is Vonnie?"

"It was very hard for her," Jimmy said, turning his face to hide his emotions. "I think she's coming to see you in a few days."

"I wish I could have been there with her," Grace said .

"She understood," Jimmy assured her. "It was a big funeral. I think Shoney's death brought sanity back to Tererro, and people realized they didn't want to fight anymore. They settled the strike yesterday, and everyone will be back on the job tomorrow. Shoney will always be a hero."

"Did you help with the negotiations?"

"I did, I'm happy to say, and the miners received a good raise and better medical benefits."

"I'm glad for everyone," Grace said with a smile. "But you've decided you don't want to be a miner anymore?"

"Well, I enjoy law enforcement, and the mine may not be in production too much longer, anyway. Ted Cooper tells me if there is another strike in the near future, the company will close it down. I guess their profit margin is pretty slim. They'll concentrate on their operation in South America where labor is cheaper."

"Well, Dad will just have to help Leota run the lodge then," Grace said with a resigned smile.

"By the way, getting back to Vonnie," Jimmy said. "I think she might want you to take over her classes. She tells me she's going back to Paris."

"I can do that," Grace said as she brushed the back of her hands over her eyes.

"But, I think she also might want you to take her classes in Santa Fe as well."

"I can probably do that, too, but I'm really going to miss her," Grace said, shaking her head sadly.

After a short silence, Jimmy changed the subject. "By the way, I caught that no good so and so and his friend."

"You mean Bill McKane?"

"Yeah. I had seen Duchess tied at the Owens' house while patrolling nearby. I stopped and asked them where you were, and they told me what had happened. I went right to Indian Cave and was there to greet McKane and his friend when they came back. I beat the bastard within an inch of his life. We think he killed Shoney and possibly Mr. Dodson. Our investigation is continuing."

"Thank you," Grace said. "I'm very proud of you."

"I'm proud of you," Jimmy said. "What a girl I've got." He raised her hand to his lips and gently kissed it. "My little Pecos Queen," he said tenderly. "You put your life on the line for all of us."

Grace nestled back into her pillows, feeling satisfied with the world right now in spite of her headache.

Mrs. Smith stuck her head into the room. "She needs her rest now, Mr. Kirkwood."

As Jimmy stood up, Grace looked admiringly at him. "You are so handsome in your uniform," she said smugly.

"I'm going to go now," Jimmy said as he planted a light kiss on her lips. "But, I'll be back later to get a statement about what happened. Then, there's another little investigation I've got to make involving a ring."

"A ring?" Grace asked coyly, her eyes sparkling.

"You heard right," Jimmy said, his face beaming. "I've got to brand the Pecos Queen so she doesn't run off with the next handsome man who wants to take her to Hollywood. Because, you're mine, Tex. All mine."

"And that's all I ever want," Grace said tenderly, tears shining in her eyes. "I want only you and your strawberry kisses forever, my love."

"I've got to go to Law Enforcement School," Jimmy said quickly. "I'll be in Santa Fe for three months, but that ring will be on your finger before I go. I promise you."

"And, there's one more important thing I've got to do," Jimmy said as he bent down to her.

"What?" Grace asked running her finger over the lips she remembered so well.

"I've got a bedroom to build," he whispered as he gently tasted the sweetness of love's passionate promise in her warmly responsive kisses.

www.ingramcontent.com/pod-product-compliance
Lightning Source LLC
Chambersburg PA
CBHW011738010726

47496CB00010B/2994